# THE LOST CASTLE TREASURE

Sir Gregory steals the dragon's hoard

Sir Kaye, The Boy Knight® Series Book Two

# THE LOST CASTLE TREASURE

## Don M. Winn
### *Illustrated by Dave Allred*

A Cardboard Box Adventures Book

www.donwinn.com

Published 2014 by Progressive Rising Phoenix Press, LLC

www.progressiverisingphoenix.com

The characters and events portrayed in this book are fictitious. Any similarity to real persons, living or dead, is purely coincidental and not intended by the author.

Sir Kaye, the Boy Knight® is a registered trademark of Cardboard Box Adventures.

Printed in the United States of America.

*To Elizabeth*

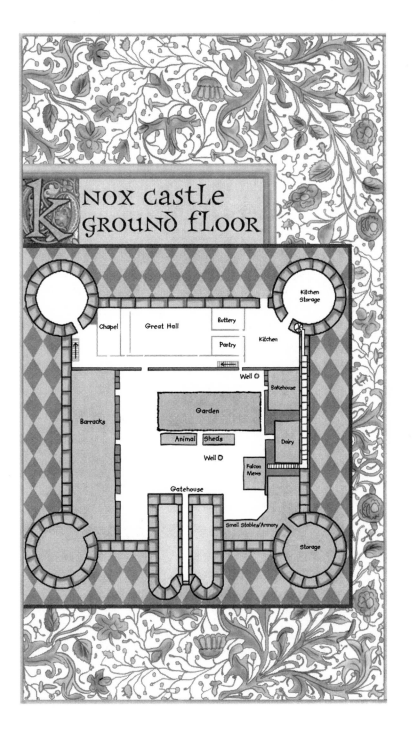

KNOX CASTLE
GROUND FLOOR

Kitchen Storage

Chapel

Great Hall

Buttery

Pantry

Kitchen

Well

Bakehouse

Garden

Barracks

Animal Sheds

Dairy

Well

Falcon Mews

Gatehouse

Small Stables/Armory

Storage

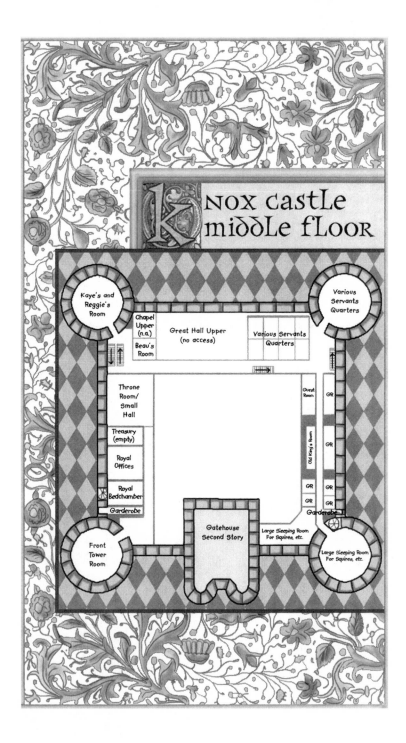

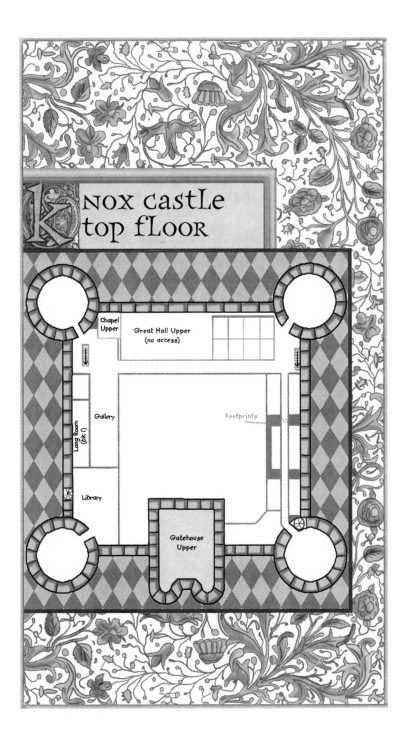

# Knox Castle
# Top Floor

Chapel
Upper

Great Hall Upper
(no access)

Gallery

Long Room
(bk 1)

Footprints

Library

Gatehouse
Upper

# pROLoGue

One black and bitter night when even the moon had gone dark, two men dragged a stumbling, gray-cloaked woman down the road from the castle. When they arrived at the gatehouse, the shorter man shoved open the heavy doors facing the main road. The other man tossed the old woman to the ground. The sneer on his handsome face deepened as her knees hit the hard earth with a thud.

"Get out, old woman. You're not welcome here," the short man said, laughing until he started coughing. He sounded like he was choking. "Curse this cold weather," he muttered once he caught his breath.

The woman begged, "Please, oh, please, Sir Knights, it *is* cold. Don't throw me out. I'm all alone. I've nothing left but my bones."

The handsome knight smoothed back his wavy hair and said, "Nothing left, eh? Let's see. You might be right." He started counting on his fingers. "No husband, right?"

She stared at him in shock.

"True," the choking knight said. "He's dead. Quite dead."

A fire began to kindle in the woman's pale eyes.

The handsome knight continued, leaning elegantly against the gatehouse doorway. "No king."

The choking knight laughed until he had another coughing fit. When he could speak again, he said, "That's right. The king's dead too. But you know that," he said, leaning over the woman. "You watched him die. You couldn't do anything to save him, could you?"

The fire in her eyes disappeared as the woman began to cry without a sound.

"It's cold," the handsome knight said with a yawn and a shiver. "I'm going back inside." He nudged the woman out of the doorway with his foot. "Be gone, old woman. Never show your face here again!"

The knights crashed the doors shut in her face. She tottered to her feet, only to wander through the village crying out, "Please, have pity on an old woman! Have mercy!" over and over again. No one heard her frail cries for help. Exhausted, she spent the rest of the night in a ditch, huddled under a pile of dry leaves. At first light she turned her back on the village, realizing there was only one place left for her to go.

"You won't be rid of me that easy, you filthy knights," she muttered. "You robbed me of everything I loved—my home—my husband—even my king. You'll pay for this!" She set off across the fields, disappearing into the thick morning fog.

# CHAPTER ONE

Our horses' hooves left trails of puddles as we plodded along the rain-soaked path. Dripping leaves scattered us with icy drops, making me glad I wore a thick wool cloak. Outside, I felt cold and wet and uncomfortable, but inside I buzzed with happiness like bees in a hive of fresh honey. My best friend Kaye and I were on our way to live at the queen's castle, and that could mean only one thing—adventure!

"Are we almost there? I'm so excited! Aren't you excited?" I asked, forgetting that Kaye already lived in a castle. His father was Sir Henry Balfour, the greatest knight in Knox. I lived in the town of Crofton, where my father was a wool merchant.

"Yes, of course," Kaye said. He rubbed his chin hard, which meant he was thinking.

"What's wrong?" I asked.

Alfred frowned at me. He never spoke, but I knew he wanted me to be quieter. Bandits lurked along every road in Knox, and Alfred's job was to deliver us safely to the castle.

"The other knights at the castle won't be happy to see me again. Most of them hate me," Kaye said.

He was right. A few weeks ago, the new queen of Knox had knighted Kaye for rescuing her nephew. At first, the knights only laughed at the idea of a twelve-year-old knight, but after Kaye defeated the great Sir Melchor in a tournament contest, they hated him—especially Sir Melchor and his friends.

"Do you think they'll beat you up?" I asked, feeling worried. The other knights were much bigger than Kaye.

"I hope not!" he said. "I was just thinking that if the other knights hate me, I can never be a truly good knight. Nobody hates the good knights. Everyone still loves Sir Gregory—and he's been dead for probably a hundred years. People love my father too. I want to be like that so I can help people, and I want my father to be proud of me when he comes back." Sir Henry had been in the neighboring kingdom of Eldridge for two years now, working to keep peace between the two countries.

I snorted. "Your father is always proud of you. Be glad you don't have my father. He's never proud of me. I'm not good at anything. I think he would like me better if I were a sheep. At least then he could sell my wool."

Alfred—Kaye and I secretly called him Old Stone Face—gave a little grunt and stared at me with that blank look cows have when they chew. Tiny drops of mist coated his long beard until it glittered with silver. I blushed, feeling like Alfred had just yelled at me for being rude about my father. "Sorry," I muttered. "I just wish—"

I was interrupted by a noise that sounded like a little axe whacking sharply into a tree. I wondered if there were woodcutters nearby.

Kaye yanked out his sword and sent his horse Kadar crashing into the dense bushes along the trail. Alfred followed close behind him. Confused, I blinked and looked around. I saw that a single dark arrow had bitten deep into a tree just above my head. Kaye and Alfred had gone after the archer and left me alone.

I heard a faint scraping noise above me, and saw something roll off the branches above. It was about the size of a small squirrel and attached to a string like a spider. The spider-squirrel fell until it stopped with a bounce, dangling over the path in front of me.

I rode a few steps forward to look at the thing more closely. When I saw what it was, my chest froze over with fear. It felt like hundreds of tiny jagged icicles stabbing at me every time my heart decided to thump. After a few moments, Kaye and Alfred finally reappeared on the path some distance behind me.

"The mystery archer is gone," Kaye said, riding closer. "I guess I won't be needing this after all." His green eyes glinted with the same light that ran down the blade of his sword as he put it away. His ginger hair made a spot of bright color against the gray forest, and when he pushed back his cloak, I saw that he was wearing a brown shirt with his knight's crest on it—a white eagle against a blue shield.

"Kaye. Look," I said, croaking like an old frog. I pointed at the thing swaying gently on its string.

It was a little man made of sticks with a tuft of orange wool stuck to its head. On its chest was a blue smear. On top of the blue smear was a white bird. And wrapped around its neck was a hangman's noose.

This time my voice came out high and squeaky, like I didn't have enough air. "Kaye, we can't go to the castle; it's too dangerous. Someone wants you dead!"

Kaye didn't answer. He stared at the branch above the stick man and then moved his gaze over to the arrow embedded in the tree.

"Kaye! What are you doing? We should go home!"

Kaye grabbed my shoulder and shook me a little bit. "Calm down, Reggie. Look at this." He took my horse's bridle and led me over to the arrow.

"See what happened?" he asked. I shook my head.

"Someone made the stick man look like it was being hanged. Then he tied the stick man high out of sight with another rope and tied *that* rope around this tree. When we came along, he shot the rope, broke it, and the stick man fell down in front of us. It's a simple trick, really."

"A simple trick!" I cried. "Someone's trying to kill you!"

"I don't think so," he said. "He's only trying to scare us."

"How do you know?"

Kaye pointed to a slim piece of rope pinned to the tree trunk by the dark arrow. "Because the archer hit this skinny rope with one shot. Do you know how hard it is to hit a target that small—especially on a misty day like today?"

I nodded. I liked archery, but I knew that even with years of practice, I would never hit a tiny rope like that with an arrow. "So?" I asked.

He shrugged. "He must be one of the best archers in Knox. If someone that good with a bow really wants me dead, he would shoot at me instead of a tree. It's faster than making a stick man and climbing around tying ropes to branches."

I calmed down a little. "Maybe," I said, "but it's not fair! I thought we'd have fun and adventure at the castle, not enemies. We should go back home. Our mums would want us to."

"Adventures aren't always fun," Kaye said. "Sometimes they're really uncomfortable, but I can't go back now. I'll never become the kind of knight I need to be by staying home. If you want to go home, we'll take you, but I have to go on."

I thought about home. I missed my mum a lot, but I knew what waited for me there—learning to be a boring wool merchant and frustrating my father every day by failing at everything. If

I was ever going to find out what I was good at, I had to go on to the castle with Kaye.

"I'll go with you," I said. "I'd rather be stuck full of arrows than become a wool merchant anyway."

Kaye laughed and waved at Alfred, who waited patiently in the middle of the path. "Come on, Alfred," Kaye cried, "we're going to the castle!" Kaye seized the dangling puppet with one hand, and his sword sang as he unsheathed it and sliced through the string. He threw the stick man to the ground and we trampled it to splinters as we galloped onward through the mist.

# chapter two

Late in the afternoon, we entered a large, sleepy village. Houses and shops clustered tightly around the road like gossiping old women.

Beyond the village, Castle Forte's outer wall loomed through the thinning fog, rooted deep in the ground like a mountain and as thick as three tall men laid end to end. Narrow slits for archers studded the massive towers, and iron bars strengthened the heavy oak doors of the gatehouse. These doors stood wide open, but as we entered, a whiny voice called out, "Welcome, Sir Milksop!"

Two knights lounged in the shadows just inside the tunnel-like passage leading through the gatehouse. I knew them as friends of Sir Melchor. The whiny-voiced Sir Oliphus was as skinny as a weasel and as sour-faced as the smell of spoiled milk. His flat, yellow fingers fiddled with a bundle of stained rags wrapped around his right knee. The other knight, a thick-muscled, long-armed, young fellow, stood and stretched, then slung a quiver of arrows over his shoulder. His patchy beard looked like a moldy old wolf skin stuck to his face.

Kaye sat up as straight as if he had an iron spike in his back instead of bones. "Good morrow, Sir Oliphus," he said pleasantly. "I trust the queen is in good health. Is there any news?"

Both knights glared at him. Sir Oliphus replied, "News? Of course there's news. Our neighbor Eldridge is about to break into civil war. The price of wool is up, although sheep are reported missing in the north. And, oh yes, an upstart *speck* of a boy is playing at being a knight of Knox and embarrassing us all!"

"What?" the other knight cried out in pretend shock. "Show him to me! I'll teach him to respect his elders. When I finish with him, he won't insult us by pretending to be one of us!"

Kaye's knuckles whitened as he clenched his horse's reins. Villagers appeared out of nowhere, gathering around to watch the long-armed knight put on a show. He pulled an arrow from his quiver, set it to his bow, and began hopping and creeping around like a hunter searching for prey. He looked like an actor from a traveling play on a festival day.

The villagers laughed as he sighted along the arrow at Alfred, shook his head and turned away. He tiptoed around Kaye's horse, ducked sideways, and suddenly stood up with his shoulder directly under Kaye's foot, heaving Kaye to the ground. I winced as Kaye landed on his knee and elbow. The knight whirled around and pointed the arrow in Kaye's face. "Is this the villain you spoke of?" he growled to Sir Oliphus.

Sir Oliphus pushed his moldy-faced friend aside. "Now, Sir Milo, don't you recognize the most famous knight in Knox? He defeated Sir Melchor at the last tournament, in a peculiar contest designed so that only he could win."

Grabbing Kaye by the arm, Oliphus pulled him to his feet. "Oh-ho, what's this I feel?" he said. "I think that Sir Milksop's sword arm has grown stronger since his last visit. Perhaps he is finally ready to battle the beetles and fleas that plague this castle."

"Only if he fights the beetles one at a time," Milo said. "If he fought them all at once, they would surely defeat him!" Everyone roared with laughter. Sir Milo bowed to the villagers, rudely bumping Kaye with his backside and knocking Kaye to the ground again.

One of the villagers called out, "Not much of a knight, is he? Can't seem to stand up for himself!"

Kaye's face turned red with cheese-colored blotches as everyone howled with laughter. Milo guffawed, strode over to the man, and flung his arm around his shoulders. "Here is a good fellow," he shouted. "Come, friend, I will buy you some ale!" He looked around at the crowd and held up a small purse that jingled. "Ale for everyone! A gift from Sir Melchor to his friends!" The crowd cheered and followed him to the village alehouse.

Sir Oliphus coughed and spat toward Kaye. A yellow blob landed in the crumbling mud next to Kaye's knee as Oliphus growled, "You're not wanted here, boy. Take your brat face and your brat friend and go home. Castles are dangerous places for those who don't belong there."

He limped after the others, leaving the three of us alone in the dark tunnel.

I got off my horse and ran to Kaye. "Are you hurt?"

He stood up and rubbed his elbow. "I'm fine," he said, using his toe to cover Oliphus' spit with mud.

"Kaye," I said, "Are you sure you don't want to go home?"

Kaye climbed back onto his horse. "I told you, Reggie, I have to stay. They're just trying to scare me off. They'll stop bothering me once they see that it doesn't work. Maybe I can even win them over in time."

"How? They hate you."

He shrugged. "I don't know, but I'll think of something. Maybe if I do something important enough, they'll stop hating me."

Alfred boosted me back onto my horse. As we passed through the outer wall and started up the road to the castle, Kaye said, "Did you see Sir Milo's arrows? They were dark, just like the arrow in the forest."

Alfred grunted in agreement, but I shivered and said nothing. This castle was built of strong stone and iron and wood. It could protect us from enemies outside its walls, but what would save us from the enemies inside?

# chapter three

After passing through the gatehouse of the inner wall, we saw Duke Beauregard, the queen's nephew, waiting for us in the courtyard. A bird with its head covered up sat on his fist. Happy to see a friendly face, Kaye and I called out, "Beau!" Alfred gave us a good-bye snort and headed for the stables.

"Kaye! Reggie! I'm glad you've arrived safely," Beau said. "Come meet Oriana, but be quiet. She's jumpy today."

"So am I," I said, tumbling off my horse.

"What's wrong?" Beau asked. "You look funny."

"Lots of things. Like someone shot at us in the forest," I said, getting upset all over again.

"What?" Beau cried. "What villain did that?"

Kaye swung off Kadar and said, "Well, someone shot an arrow, but it wasn't exactly aimed at us." I waited for him to finish the story, but all he said was, "Tell us about Oriana."

I couldn't believe it. Someone had shot at us and pretended to hang Kaye. The queen's own knights had hurt and humiliated him right outside the castle, but he acted like nothing was wrong.

"Sounds like an accident," Beau said. "I'm glad no one was hurt. Look here." He held his bird out toward us. Her smooth, curved talons clutched at the thick leather gauntlet that protected Beau's hands. A hood covered her eyes. "This is Oriana, my goshawk. I'll never starve as long as I have her—she's the best hunter I've ever seen."

"She's beautiful," Kaye said. "My father used to hunt with a falcon." He paused a moment and the excitement faded from his eyes. He looked down and continued, "He was going to teach me, but he never did. He went to Eldridge instead."

"I'll teach you," Beau said cheerfully. "It will be fun. I'm glad there will be falcons living in the mews again."

"What are the mews?" I asked.

Beau pointed to the stone building behind him. "It's where the falcons and hunting hawks live. Let's go in. The old king kept beautiful gyrfalcons here, but they disappeared when he got sick. I suppose they were stolen."

Kaye whistled. "They must have been worth more gold than I'll ever see."

The falcon mews was a big, empty room, with perches of different sizes all over the wood-paneled walls. Loose gravel covered the ground. In the dim light, I saw fancy letters carved over the perches, but they were too curly to read. I reached up with one finger and touched the closest one, but all I could figure out was that the first letter was a D.

Beau stood nearby, curiously watching me feel the letters. I blushed. "What does it say?" I asked.

"That one says Delilah. I think the carvings are the names of the falcons who lived here," Beau said, "but they're old and hard to read. I can't figure out any of the others."

"Oh, right. I can't either," I said, feeling glad I wasn't the only one who had trouble reading the carvings.

Back in the courtyard, Beau said, "You missed the excitement this morning. One of the knights broke into the queen's apartments and burned some of the old king's private notes and letters. Now he's locked in one of the towers."

"Did he burn anything important?" Kaye asked.

Beau shrugged. "The queen isn't familiar with all the old king's things yet, so she has no idea what's missing."

I shivered again and said, "None of the knights here are up to any good."

Beau patted my shoulder. "They're not all bad, Reggie. Sir Griswald's a decent fellow. He likes Oriana. Would you like to hold her?" he asked, trying to cheer me up.

I had never seen Beau look happier than he did with that bird on his fist. His eyes were clear and blue like the queen's, and today they shone as bright as his smile always did.

Beau pulled the hood off Oriana's head. I felt like her sharp golden eyes saw straight through me to all my soft insides. I probably looked like a tasty treat to her.

Backing up, I bumped against Kadar and said, "Um, maybe later." I'd never been this close to a bird of prey before. My heart clanged louder than a blacksmith's hammer. Kadar kindly stepped between me and Oriana.

Kaye took three steps forward. "I'd love to hold her!"

Beau pointed to a spare gauntlet. "Put that on first."

Kaye put on the heavy glove. Beau held his hand just below Kaye's, and Oriana stepped up to the higher perch. She clenched her powerful feet around Kaye's hand until I worried she would pinch it in two, but Kaye wasn't bothered at all.

"She's amazing!" Kaye said. "She's so strong."

Beau smiled at his bird and said, "I'm glad you like her. You can help me fly her." He looked at me and added, "You too, Reggie, because soon I'll have another falcon! When my aunt became queen, she made me a duke, and now I can fly a peregrine falcon. I have an expert falconer to help me train her and—"

Beau suddenly stopped talking. "I shouldn't say anything else or I'll spoil the surprise."

"What surprise?" we shouted. Oriana ruffled her feathers and glared at us—at me, mostly. She seemed to like Kaye.

"It's good news," Beau said, "but the queen wants to tell you herself. So take care of your horses, and we'll go up to your room. She'll come find us there."

Kaye and I crossed the courtyard to the stables. As we settled our horses in their stalls I said, "Kaye, why didn't you tell Beau what really happened in the forest?"

Kaye looked around. No one was near, but he lowered his voice and said, "I think Milo shot the arrow. If we tell everyone about it, he'll know it upset me. I'm hoping he'll leave me alone if I ignore him."

When we finished, the three of us entered the castle and climbed the main staircase. Our room was in one of the second-floor towers, close to Beau's room and not far from the queen's chambers.

"Your room is exactly the way you left it," Beau said, "including a full chamber pot." We all laughed until one by one, we stopped laughing and gave each other puzzled looks as we sniffed the air.

"What's that foul stench?" I bleated, pinching my nose shut.

"It's coming from the tower room," Kaye said, sniffing in that direction.

"I was only joking about the chamber pot," Beau said. As we entered the room, we saw the cause of the stink. Mounds of sticky-looking brown ooze erupted over the formerly white bedcover and dribbled down the sides of the wooden bed.

"Ugh!" Beau said. "Someone filled your bed with disgusting drippy pig muck!"

# chapter four

"Who did this?" I cried, although I thought I already knew the answer.

"I don't know," Beau said, "but let's clean this up before the queen comes. I'll get a bucket." He disappeared into the passage. I didn't blame him. The stink was awful. If I had known where to find a bucket, I would have been the first to go get one.

"Well, Reggie, it looks like you have the first deposit for your pigge pot," Kaye said.

I frowned. A pigge pot was just an ordinary kitchen jar made of clay. Sometimes people kept their coins in a pigge pot. "Huh?" I said. "I don't have any money."

I didn't have a pigge pot either, but that was beside the point. I squinted at Kaye, growing suspicious. "Are you making another bad joke?"

"Yes," Kaye said with glee. "Because there's a *deposit* on the bed. And it came from a pig." He set down his small bag of belongings and said, "Never mind. Let's look around here for any other—presents."

He looked in the wardrobe. "Empty," he said.

I dropped my own bag on the floor and peered under the bed. "There's nothing here but the chamber pot." I pulled it out, lifted the lid, and looked inside. "It's empty too, and probably cleaner than the rest of the room," I said, holding the pot upside down over my head.

Beau returned with two big buckets and Nicolette, the queen's lady-in-waiting. She gasped and covered her nose and mouth with her hands.

Beau laughed out loud. "Reggie! You look so funny, staring up into a chamber pot. I would give good gold to see that as a wood carving! It would be one of my most treasured possessions."

I narrowed my eyes at him. "I'm glad you see something funny about all this," I said, setting the pot down.

"Oh, no, there is nothing funny," Nicolette said, lifting a perfumed pomander ball to her nose. "This is dreadful. When Beau told me about the mess, I thought, yes, maybe there will be a little dirt, but this—this is so very ugly and wet!" She looked like she was about to cry, but maybe it was the hideous smell that brought the water to her eyes.

We dumped the filthy slop in the garden and stuffed a clean bed sack with fresh straw to make a new mattress. As soon as we finished, Queen Vianne entered the room, wrinkling her nose a tiny bit. I guess the smell wasn't completely gone. Kaye and I immediately dropped to our knees, saying, "Your Majesty!"

The queen regarded us with calm blue eyes. Her dark hair framed her serious face and made her skin look like white ivory, despite the purple smudges under her eyes. Even though she was small and young, she stood up straight and dignified, just like a queen should. Her smiles shone warmer than summer.

"Welcome, Kaye and Reggie," she said. "Please rise. Remember you are family here. You don't have to be so formal when we're alone."

It was hard not to be formal around the queen, but I tried leaning against the bed post. That seemed to work. Kaye looked at the queen expectantly.

"I'm sorry about your bed. This is not the welcome I wanted for you, but I hope you know that both Beau and I are very glad you're here."

"Thank you, Your Majesty!" I said.

Kaye looked serious. "We're glad to be here, Your Majesty."

The queen smiled and said, "I'm happy to hear that. I also have a lovely surprise for you! There is someone I want you to meet soon. His name is Alchir, and he was my tutor in Vinland when I was younger. Now he'll be your tutor."

"He's a master falconer too," Beau added. "He's the one that helped me train Oriana."

"He's a scholar, teacher, and falconer," the queen said. "He will live here and tutor you for three hours each morning. You'll love him, I promise."

I felt like a mace had smashed into my chest. I couldn't breathe. My knees stopped working and I sat down hard on the bed behind me. I would have done it even if it had still been covered with pig muck.

"A tutor?" I whispered.

Nobody noticed me because Kaye was shouting, "Thank you, Your Majesty! What a wonderful surprise. Now I can learn how to hunt with a falcon just like my father!"

"Of course you can," Beau said with a big smile, "You'll be good at it too, I can tell."

"There's more to learn than falconry," the queen said. "Alchir will teach you many things."

Everyone looked at me expectantly. I had to say something. I couldn't say what I really felt, especially to the queen. She was so happy her face glowed like a new candle. I didn't want to be the scoundrel who blew that candle out.

I licked my lips and took a deep breath. "Um, thank you, Your Majesty," I said. "My father will be so pleased to know I will learn from the queen's own tutor."

The queen smiled and said, "I'm happy to hear that, Reggie. You must write and tell him about it. And now, after such a long journey, you must be hungry. The great hall is repaired and the kitchen boys are about to serve dinner. Why don't you go see what Abelard has cooked tonight? I'll join you soon." She headed down the hall to her own rooms.

The four of us followed her advice. I walked with Nicolette because I needed information. She kept lifting her pomander ball to her nose. Finally she dropped it with a big sigh. "Nothing works," she said. "The bad smell stays in my nose."

I sniffed the air. There *was* a faint scent of pig everywhere.

Nicolette offered me her pomander ball. "Maybe it will work for you," she said as we reached the top of the stairs. "Put it up to your nose and smell."

Kaye and Beau went down, but Nicolette waited so I could try her pomander. It was an elegant hollow silver ball hanging by a chain from her belt.

I sniffed at it. Something inside smelled like a whole field of flowers on a sunny afternoon. I could have smelled it all day long, but I felt funny sniffing it while it was still attached to Nicolette, so I handed it back to her. "Thank you," I said. "It helped. Can I—can I ask you something?"

She nodded, so I asked, "Do you know the queen's tutor?"

"Alchir? Yes, I have known him for many years," she said.

"What's he like?" I asked.

She shrugged. "He knows many things. The queen and Beau are very fond of him."

"But is he good?" I asked. "Is he kind?"

She laughed a tinkling laugh. "He will not beat you, if that is what makes you worry."

"Who says I'm worrying?" I said, sticking my chin out.

Nicolette lightly brushed the frown between my eyebrows with her finger. "Your face is worried," she said.

"It's because it knows I'm stupid," I said before I could stop myself.

"Your face is wrong," she whispered. "I know that you are not stupid." She patted my cheek and went downstairs. I sighed and followed her. I didn't want to go anywhere I might meet the tutor, but I was hungry, and my stomach pulled me straight down toward the food like a stone dropped into a pond.

# chapter five

Kaye and Beau were waiting for me at the bottom of the stairs. Before we could follow Nicolette into the great hall, Melchor came in from the courtyard. His brushy black beard prickled like a hedgehog's back and his big belly hung over his belt. He still dressed in brown wool and leather like a common villager.

"Ah, Sir Kaye," he said in a hearty voice, "you're back again—so soon. I heard you received a warm welcome from Sir Milo today."

He stepped toward us. I jumped, but Kaye gazed calmly at Melchor before nodding, "Yes, I met Sir Milo when I arrived."

"Sir Milo is a fine and worthy knight," Melchor said. "He was my squire before he was knighted, you know. He's like a son to me. A good son, who respects me like a father."

"The villagers like him very much," Kaye said politely.

"Yes," Melchor said. "Too bad they don't feel the same about you. But people know so little about you. You simply appeared one day as the queen's new favorite. No wonder the people are suspicious of you—and the queen."

"There's nothing to be suspicious about," Kaye said. "My father is Sir Henry. Everyone in Knox knows him. They trust him."

"Do they really trust him?" Melchor asked. "He's been gone a long time. People say he's become the close friend of the king of Eldridge. They say he makes his pockets fat with gold by selling our secrets to the king."

I stared at Melchor. Was he crazy? No one thought that about Sir Henry. Then I realized he was trying to make Kaye mad. It worked. Kaye turned bright red, whipped out his sword, and cried, "How dare you say those things about my father? He's more loyal to Knox than you'll ever be!"

Melchor laughed. The sound was slow and comfortable, like he enjoyed it. "Loyal? I'm loyal. I'm the best knight in Knox, and unlike your father, I am here to support my queen."

Kaye brandished his sword, too angry to speak. Melchor backed away from Kaye and pulled out his own sword. It made a metallic scraping noise that seemed to go on forever.

"Melchor." Beau spoke in a stern voice. "The queen will be most displeased if you hurt Kaye."

Melchor grinned and wagged his beard at Beau. Then he swung the tip of his sword around and around in a twisted circle that got bigger and bigger, moving faster and faster. Suddenly, Melchor changed his grip on the handle and launched the sword toward Kaye like a spear. It flew through the air and landed upright with its point stuck between two stones. The sword was almost taller than Kaye.

"Young Balfour," he said, "Do not wave your sword at me again. You don't want to cross blades with me in a real fight. Next time, I might stab more than the stones."

Kaye didn't back down as Melchor loomed closer. He glared at Melchor, clutching his sword hilt so hard his hand shook. "My father's not a traitor!" he said. "People shouldn't say such things about him!"

"No?" Melchor asked. "Do you know what they say about you?" His hand darted like a striking snake and grabbed Kaye by the collar. Melchor lifted Kaye until he could see straight into his eyes. Kaye dropped his sword with a clang onto the stones below.

Melchor smiled. "They say you're working with your father, a spy tucked neatly into the castle, sent to betray the queen and all her secrets to Eldridge."

"You lie! The queen is my friend. I wouldn't betray her!" Kaye kicked sharply at Melchor's fat stomach as his face turned purple with anger and choking.

I ran to Melchor and grabbed his belt with both hands. I tried to shake him so he'd let go of Kaye, but I only ended up shaking myself back and forth. Melchor swept me aside with his free hand, and I hit the ground just as the door to the courtyard flew open.

Milo stepped inside, saying, "Melchor, they brought your new horse. I never saw a better one—" He finally noticed Kaye in the air and his lips curled into an ugly smile. "I see you're busy," he said.

The neck of Kaye's tunic gave way with a ripping noise. Kaye landed on the floor, and Melchor towered over him, scowling. "Go home, little spy," he said. "Go home before you make people hate your father even more."

Melchor picked up his sword, turned to leave, and stumbled over me. For once, he forgot to keep his smile on, screaming, "You! What *are* you? At least your fine friend Balfour pretends to be a knight. You do nothing. You're like a dog's tail. All you do is follow the dog around. Useless trash!" Melchor stormed past Milo into the courtyard, hollering, "Where's my horse?"

Milo smirked and jabbed me in the ribs with the toe of his muddy boot. "Get up Dogtail. Go home. You too, Sir Spy. You've wasted enough of Melchor's time." Milo left, slamming the heavy door behind him.

# CHAPTER SIX

Kaye stomped over to where his sword lay on the ground. He snatched it up and shoved it back into its sheath. Then he paced back and forth, fuming and muttering under his breath. I had never seen him so angry.

I slipped my hand into my pocket and found an old glass bead. I held it tight while I lay there hating Melchor and Milo. They were so mean. Melchor always knew just the right thing to say to hurt someone.

Beau came over to help me up. "Don't listen to Melchor," he said. "He's wrong. And anyway, the tail is the friendliest part of a dog. That makes it the best part."

I smiled half-heartedly. Beau meant well, but he didn't know Melchor was right about me. I wasn't good at anything.

Kaye stomped over to us, saying, "How dare he call my father a traitor! Do people really think that?"

"No," I said, "but what were you thinking? Why did you pull a sword on Melchor? He could have killed you!"

Kaye snorted. "He won't hurt me. He wants people to think he's a perfect knight."

"Maybe," I said, "but he knows how to make you angry enough to do something really stupid—like pulling a sword on the biggest, strongest knight in Knox. Be careful."

"Reggie's right," Beau said. "You should stay away from Melchor."

"I can't do that!" Kaye shouted in exasperation. "If I stay away, it looks like I have something to hide. If people really think my father and I are spies and traitors, I have to show them they're wrong. I have to do something!"

"What?" Beau asked.

Kaye scrunched up his face. "I don't know," he admitted. "But I'll think of something—something big."

"What's wrong?" the queen asked, coming down the staircase.

Kaye looked embarrassed, but Beau said, "Melchor says Sir Henry is a traitor and Kaye is a spy. Kaye wants to prove him wrong."

"Kaye," the queen said, "please don't listen to Melchor. I trust your father and I trust you. If you want to prove Melchor wrong, it will take time—time for you to grow in your knowledge and skills, and time for people to get to know you and trust you."

"Yes, Your Majesty," Kaye said, "but how are they going to get to know me if I don't *do* anything?"

The queen sighed. I didn't blame her. Kaye could be very stubborn. "Why don't we talk about this over dinner?" she said, leading us into the great hall.

The great hall looked much better than it did the first time we visited the castle. The huge room was swept clean, with fresh rushes spread over the stone floor. The garbage piles and broken furniture had vanished. At one end of the hall, a long table on a raised platform waited for the queen.

Instead of going to the high table, Queen Vianne led us to a white-covered table near one of the fireplaces. "Tonight we'll eat alone," she said. "I haven't invited the knights to join me in the hall yet."

Soon the kitchen boys carried in plate after plate of food, almost more than I could count. They brought roast pig with an apple in its mouth and mutton and spiced wine and bread and cheese and custard and soup and pickled herring and lots of other things.

It smelled so good! I ate two helpings of everything, piling the food high on my trencher, but Kaye was deep in thought. With his elbow on the table, he held up his head by grabbing a handful of his own hair and leaning on his clenched fist. He stared straight into the little brown roasted piggy face in front of him, but saw nothing. Beau caught my eye and rolled his own eyes all the way up to the high vaulted ceiling of the hall.

Queen Vianne and Nicolette talked together about people they knew back in Vinland. While they were busy, I picked up a pea and tossed it high in the air toward Kaye. It fell down right in front of his face, landing on his trencher. He didn't notice. I threw another one that bounced off his forehead. He didn't even blink.

Beau reached over and gently pulled the apple out of the pig's mouth. Then he wriggled the pig's jaw around until it was loose and pretended to make the pig talk to Kaye.

"Oh, Sir Kaye, I'm so sorry my muck got all over your bed," Beau spoke for the pig in a high-pitched voice. "My brother Melchor put it there. He is an embarrassment to all pigs everywhere. He wouldn't even make a good roast."

I burst out laughing, but locked in his thoughts, Kaye stared straight at the pig without noticing anything.

"What's this?" Nicolette asked.

Beau made the pig talk to her, "Oh, Lady Nicolette, pray, have some more pork."

Nicolette swatted Beau's arm and said, "Stop that! The animals should not talk. How can we eat them if they talk?"

Suddenly Kaye slapped his hand down flat on the table. "I have it! Your Majesty, I need a quest. All knights go on quests. If you send me on a mission, no one will think I am working against you."

# CHAPTER SEVEN

The queen smiled and said, "What kind of quest do you have in mind?"

"I could rescue someone," Kaye said.

"I don't know anyone who needs rescuing right now," the queen said.

"What about slaying a dragon?" I asked.

Kaye glared at me. "There haven't been dragons in Knox for hundreds of years," he said. "I need something real."

I sulked in my chair. Now Kaye didn't even like my ideas. Melchor was right. I wasn't good at anything. I didn't know why I had come to this stupid castle in the first place.

"What about delivering an important message?" Kaye asked. "I could do that. Or you could send me to find something that's been lost or stolen. Or I could be a spy *for* you."

I went back to eating. Just because Kaye was determined to find a quest right now didn't mean I had to eat cold food. I decided to try a stuffed egg.

"Kaye," the queen said, "I promised your mother that I would try to keep you safe. I can't let you go roaming around the countryside by yourself just because you want a quest."

"He doesn't have to leave the castle," Beau said. "Kaye can look for the lost treasure. Everyone else has tried. Why shouldn't he?"

Startled, my mouth popped open and I lost the bite of stuffed egg I had just taken. It landed on my trencher with a bounce and a plop. Treasure hunting? That was exactly the kind of adventure I had been hoping for ever since I knew we were going to live at the castle.

"Wait—what treasure?" Kaye said.

Beau grinned. "I knew you'd be interested. Right before the old king died, he emptied the entire treasury and hid all the money and jewels so no one could steal from him. Now that he's dead, no one knows where the treasure is."

The queen closed her eyes for a moment and rubbed her head like it hurt her. "Beau, don't get them all excited. I think the treasure was stolen. Someone must have invented the story about King Frederic hiding it to cover up the theft."

"But they left a clue!" Beau said. "Why would someone do that if they had stolen the treasure?"

"It's a terrible clue," the queen said.

"What is it?" I asked, forgetting to eat.

"Can I get it?" Beau asked the queen. She nodded. He winked at Nicolette as he wedged the apple back into the pig's mouth before leaving. Nicolette rolled her eyes.

After a moment, Kaye asked the queen, "If the treasury is empty, how can you run a country with no money?"

"It's not easy," the queen said. "Fortunately, there have been good harvests this year. I've been able to add a little money to the treasury. But we cannot afford any surprises." The queen shivered a bit and pulled her chair closer to the fire.

"Are you ill, Your Majesty?" Nicolette asked.

"No, but I have a bit of a chill and a headache," Queen Vianne replied. "I sat up too late painting last night."

The queen liked to paint. I remembered her painting designs on the walls of the tower room last time we visited the castle. I wondered what she had been painting last night, but I was afraid to ask. Maybe it was none of my business.

"Kaye," the queen said, "I'm expecting a messenger from Eldridge in the next day or so. He will bring letters from your father. If you like, you can send a letter back with the messenger."

"Thank you, Your Majesty," Kaye said.

Beau returned, carrying a small red box that held a folded parchment. He handed it to Kaye.

Kaye opened it and stared at it. He turned it upside-down. Then he turned it a quarter-turn to the left. Then he tilted his head to the right. "What is it supposed to be?" he asked.

"Let me see!" I cried. Kaye was leaning toward Beau, so I couldn't look over his shoulder.

"It's a terrible clue, isn't it?" Beau said. "All the knights in the castle have tried to find the treasure, but they got frustrated and started ripping things apart. That's why the castle was such a mess when we arrived here."

"Can I see the clue now?" I asked.

"Yes, but it won't do any good," Kaye said, giving it to me.

I glared at him and grabbed it out of his hand. I'd show him. I hoped I could look at it and know right away where to find the treasure. In a few short minutes we'd pull it out of its hiding place and Kaye would have to find some other quest.

Then I looked at the parchment. The clue *was* terrible. King Frederic had stamped his royal seal on the clue, so I knew it came from him, but I couldn't make any sense out of it. It looked like someone had drawn some squiggly lines and then sneezed ink all over them. Or like a mouse had taken an ink bath and then rolled around on the parchment to dry off. I even thought I saw something that looked like a little mouse footprint.

"Look for the treasure all you like," the queen said to Kaye, "but please wait until after your lessons each day."

"Yes, Your Majesty," Kaye said with a grin. "I can't wait to find that treasure for you."

"Don't be too confident," Beau said. "No one else has been able to find it."

"I have all the time in the world," Kaye said. "If I keep looking, I'm sure to find it someday."

At the top of the page, a few thin, shaky words looked like they were written with a spider's leg instead of a pen. I squinted at it, but I couldn't read it. The flickering light from the fire made the letters dance on the page. Holding the clue firmly against the table so nothing would move, I peered hard at the letters. I saw the queen's name, and what I guessed was the word "treasure" and the word "safe," but the writing only seemed to show that the picture *was* the clue. I held it up to the firelight, in case I could see through the splotch of ink. Nothing. I traced the squiggly lines of the drawing with my finger, in case I could recognize it as a familiar shape. Still nothing.

I sighed and handed it back. I was a fool to think I could find the treasure. Suddenly, the idea of eating didn't sound so good. I pushed my trencher away and stared into the air. After a minute, I pulled the bead out of my pocket and began twisting the edge of the tablecloth around it.

Waking from my daydream, I heard Beau say, "Lessons start tomorrow. After dinner I'll take you to meet Alchir. He's probably in the mews with Oriana now."

Ugh. Meeting the tutor would make an already terrible day even worse. I started eating again, very slowly.

"I can't wait," Kaye said, eating faster. When he and Beau finished, they stared at me in surprise.

"What?" I asked, feeling annoyed.

"Are you sick?" Kaye asked. "I've never seen you eat so slowly before."

"I'm fine," I said. "I'm just enjoying the food. You don't have to wait. Go without me." I took a big helping of custard. I really wasn't hungry, but I knew the custard would slide easily down my throat whether I was hungry or not.

"Are you sure?" Beau asked.

"Yes, I'll be done soon," I said, and finally they left me in peace.

# chapter eight

I had no intention of going to the mews. I planned to get lost in this huge castle so I wouldn't have to meet the tutor. Even better than that, I could do what I liked best—exploring! Maybe I could find the treasure, or at least something that would explain the clue.

When I finished my custard, I said good night to the queen and Nicolette and went up to our room. It smelled much better—only a little bit like pig. I grabbed a candle in a holder, found some stairs, and climbed to the third floor.

At the top of the stairs, I heard queer rustling and scratching noises in the walls. *Must be mice*, I thought to myself. I realized the foggy mist we had traveled through all day had finally pulled itself together into a real thunderstorm. I laughed, feeling pretty smart for staying indoors, because Kaye and Beau were probably getting soaked out by the mews.

As I explored, I found a long room full of suits of armor and statues. Paintings hanging on the wood-paneled walls looked like kings—probably former kings of Knox. I wondered which one was King Frederic. The long room ended in front of two beautifully carved wooden doors. All castles have secrets, and as I put my hand on the door pull, I knew I was about to discover something special about Castle Forte.

I heaved the door open. It made a horrible screech that echoed all the way down the hall while my heart turned over like a cartwheel in my chest. Stepping cautiously inside, I passed under the watchful gaze of a large wooden falcon perched over the door. I tiptoed a little further into the room, lifted my candle high in the air, and turned in a big circle. I had found the library!

Bookshelves lined all the walls. Stairs led up to a balcony, and there were more bookshelves up there, draped with thick cobwebs, each one trapping years' worth of dust. Some of the shelves had collapsed, leaving books scattered everywhere.

I had never imagined so many books. In the dim light the muted colors of the leather bindings glinted here and there with touches of gold. Some of the largest windows in the castle were here in the library, above and between the bookshelves.

I looked back at the falcon carving over the door. Now I could tell she was guarding the entrance to the library. Moving around the room, I saw that she had friends—there were falcon carvings in nooks and crannies all around the top of the room, and a few carved falcon heads peeking around corners of shelves.

Someone really loved books and falcons. I thought of the old king. Maybe this was his library. I decided to come back during the day to take a better look at this interesting room, but tonight I would keep exploring.

I wandered through dark corridors and up and down stairs until I was lost. I heard the thunder outside shouting at the rain, but the thick walls of the castle made it sound more grumbly than angry.

All I could see were stone walls and wood paneling and spider webs and dust balls the size of rabbits. At one point, I climbed a narrow, twisting staircase and came out into a hall where the floor was covered with dust as thick and untouched as a fresh snowfall.

I took two steps forward and examined the perfect footprints I left in the dust. They looked good. I pressed my hands to the ground to make hand prints.

I decided to make angels in the dust. I took a big jump forward to leave enough empty space. When I landed, little waves ruffled through the top layers of dust. Lying on my back, I fanned my arms and legs around me and carefully got up. It wasn't perfect, so I jumped forward to try again and stopped in my tracks.

A set of dark footprints cut through the dust, leading from wall to wall across the fluffy floor of the hallway. They came from nowhere and went nowhere. Just then I heard a scratching noise in the walls, followed by a slight groaning sound. *That can't be mice*, I thought.

"Who's there?" I called out, only to be met by silence. "Who's there?" I called out even louder, but this time I heard a faint whispery noise and then silence. *Spooks*, I thought—*this castle has spooks!*

I was alone in the dark with nothing but dust rabbits to protect me from groaning spooks and phantom footprints. I needed to get out of there! I ran wildly back through the dark, away from the spooks and down toward humans—any humans.

# CHAPTER NINE

I rushed headlong down the stairs, blindly turning corners and crashing into walls. At the bottom of the last flight of stairs, I tripped over my feet and went rolling head over heels across the wide floor of a warm, bright room.

I was in the kitchen, and it felt like a wonderful place just then, full of busy people and warmth. I lay there a moment, wide-eyed, red-faced, and panting.

Rain fell outside an open door, bringing puffs of fresh air into the hot kitchen. The cool gusts of wind felt good on my sweaty head.

Then I saw the three kitchen boys staring at me with their mouths hanging open. They all had light brown hair and looked like broken stair steps—one was as tall as my chest, one was exactly my height, and one was about a finger-width taller.

A tall, dark-eyed man with a neat brown beard had stopped in the middle of rolling out dough on a table. It must have been Abelard, the castle cook who had followed the queen to Knox from Vinland. I hadn't met him before. I was surprised to see how young and hearty he was. He reminded me of a very clean blacksmith. He even wore the same kind of apron.

Abelard raised his eyebrows and said, "You must be Master Reggie. What brings you to my kitchen?"

"Um," I said, standing up dizzily and trying to think of a good reason to be there. "Do you have anything to eat?"

"Anything to eat!" Abelard chuckled. "There's plenty! What's your pleasure, Master Reggie? How about a slice of that cold mutton and bread over there? Help yourself."

"Thank you, sir," I said as I headed over to the mutton. "That sounds tasty."

Abelard shook his head saying, "Call me Abelard, not sir." He frowned at the kitchen boys, who were still staring at me.

"Back to work, boys, there's nothing to watch here. Now, Master Reggie, you looked like you were in a hurry to get here, and I don't think it was for the mutton. Does something have you spooked, my boy?"

I stared at Abelard in amazement. How did he know I was spooked? "Well," I said, "now that you mention it, I did hear some strange sounds."

The middle-sized kitchen boy spun around and blurted excitedly. "It's spooks, I know it! I've been hearing queer sounds too. I hear them in the walls. And it's spooks!" He had a face full of freckles.

I dropped the mutton back on the plate and tried to keep my voice steady. "You really think there are spooks in the castle? I was up on the third floor and I heard—"

"You went to the third floor?" the small boy shouted, looking truly afraid. I noticed a big tear in his shirt sleeve that dangled below his arm like a little broken wing.

The tall boy whistled, "You're even braver than Sir Kaye, Master Reggie. No one goes up there if they don't have to."

Suddenly I felt a little proud of myself. I had been brave, the kitchen boys thought so. "Well," I said, standing a little taller, "at first I thought it was mice in the walls, but then I found footprints in the dust—they came from nowhere and they stopped at a wall. Do you know why?" I asked the boys.

The little one shook his head so hard his whole body moved. "Why?" asked the freckled one.

I paused and looked each of them deep in their eyes. "The spook walked right through the wall!"

The little one breathed in sharply, and the others stepped closer together.

I could tell I had all their attention, so I kept going, "Then I heard a deep moan from inside the wall, like the spook was trying to steal my life away—" Just then a gust of wind flapped the open door sharply against the wall with a bang. The boys jumped and yelled.

Abelard interrupted. "Now, boys, that's enough talk about spooks. You tell a good tale, Master Reggie," he said. "You made my arms bump up like a fresh-plucked goose, and it's quite a feat to do that in this heat."

"You've heard strange noises too. We all have," the freckled kitchen boy said.

"Maybe," Abelard admitted, rubbing the back of his neck. "But let's not let our imaginations get the better of us. No more talk about spooks. Finish stacking that wood, Tom, and we'll get on with our business."

I looked at the freckled boy, "Your name's Tom?" I asked him. He grinned and nodded. "Yes, Master Reggie."

I shook my head. "It's just Reggie," I said. "I'm not master of anything." I looked at the other boys. "What are your names?"

The little one stared at the floor for a moment before saying, "I'm Embert, Master Reggie."

The tall one kicked him and said, "You heard him, Embert, he doesn't want to be called master." Then he stepped forward and said, "I'm Tom too."

I looked at them. "You're both named Tom?" I asked.

Abelard laughed. "Aye, there's two Toms here." His hands full of dough, he gestured with his elbow toward freckled Tom, "We call that one Tom Spot."

Tom Spot grinned again. "Because of my spots," he said with pride, turning his head to show me his face from all sides.

"You do have a lot of spots," I said.

"Aye, he's as spotted as a trout from the Knox River," Abelard said. "And just as slippery. When there's work to be done, Tom Spot's nowhere to be found. I should know. Many's the fish I've caught in the Knox River, and many's the fish that's slipped away just when I wanted him most."

"But I thought you were from Vinland," I said.

He shook his head. "Nay, my boy. I was born and bred in Knox. But I've traveled a bit. I lived in Vinland and learned to cook there, but now I'm back."

I leaned against the table and watched him cut the flat dough into big circles. "They say you came here because you love the queen," I said.

He lifted an eyebrow. "Who told you that, my boy?"

I shrugged. "People. Nicolette."

Abelard laughed a great ringing laugh and shook his head. "Nicolette loves a good romance."

"Does that mean you don't love the queen?" I asked.

He smiled to himself and gathered up his circles of dough, placing each one into a deep dish. "I didn't say that, now, did I? The queen has had her share of sorrows, more than many people. I didn't like the thought of her being alone in my home-land with no one to look out for her."

"So you came to take care of her?" I asked.

He brushed the flour from his hands like he was brushing away my questions. "Reggie, I'm a cook. How can a cook take care of a queen? All I can do is make sure she eats well, so that's what I do."

I nodded. I could tell he thought I was being nosy, so I changed the subject. "What are you making?"

His face showed me I had done the right thing as he said, "Onion and cheese tarts for your dinners tomorrow."

"Can I help?" I asked.

Just then Kaye and Beau walked into the kitchen. "There you are, Reggie! Why didn't you come join us?" Beau asked.

"Sorry. I got lost," I said with a red face.

"Lost?" Beau asked. "Where did you get lost?"

"Well," I continued, "I took a quick look at the third floor and that's where I got lost. I found the king's old library. And then I—wait a minute, how did you know I would be in the kitchen?"

"Because that's where the food is," said Kaye.

Abelard chuckled. Embert and the Toms stood together in a corner, watching Kaye and Beau with wonder and whispering together. Abelard noticed them and looked out the door to where the rain was pouring down steadily.

"Enough of this, boys. You'd best get outside and clean yourselves off." The boys groaned.

"Oh, Ratfingers," Tom Spot muttered under his breath. I tried not to laugh. I had never heard anyone use that word before.

Tall Tom complained, "It's cold out, sir."

"It's a fine summer night," Abelard replied. "You'll be warm enough. I won't have dirty children serving my food to the queen. Spread some cloths by the fire to warm and use them to dry yourselves when you're done—and Embert, fix that sleeve. It might fall in the food someday."

Embert blushed and whispered, "Yes, Master Abelard," while Tom Spot spread some empty sacks in front of the fire. Soon all three boys were outside running and shouting in the rain.

"Maybe you should go out there too, Reggie," Kaye said.

"Why? I took a bath a few weeks ago."

"Have you looked at yourself lately?" Beau asked. "You're very fluffy tonight." He plucked a tuft of dust from the back of my head. Maybe it hadn't been the best idea to roll around on the floor upstairs.

I sighed, took off my boots, stockings, and shirt, and went outdoors. The rain poured over our heads while we chased each other, yelling and sliding across the wet grass. Even though the rain was cold, my skin felt alive and tingling from all the running.

Back in front of the big kitchen fire, I dried off, put my clothes on, and said good night to Embert, Abelard, and the Toms as I headed upstairs with Kaye and Beau. I still hadn't told them about my most important discovery of the night.

"Did you know there are spooks in this castle?" I asked.

"Spooks?" Kaye repeated, rolling his eyes. "There are no such things as spooks, Reggie."

"Why do you say there are spooks?" Beau asked, but without the eye roll.

"I heard strange sounds up on the third floor, and I saw footprints in the dust where a spook had walked through a wall, across a hall, and through another wall. Do you believe in spooks, Beau?" I asked.

"I don't know," he said. "I haven't noticed anything odd around here, but I've heard others talk about hearing strange noises."

"Whatever it is," Kaye said, "it's not spooks. I'm sure of that."

"How can you be so sure?" I said, glaring at him. He was starting to annoy me almost as much as my soggy under-breeches were annoying me. As I was climbing the stairs, they were climbing my backside.

"Because spooks are just a lot of nonsense."

"It's not nonsense!" I said. "I've heard stories and I even heard spooky noises tonight myself."

"Those are just made-up stories, Reggie," Kaye said. "And if a spook could walk through walls without leaving a mark, why would it leave footprints? It doesn't make sense."

He stumped me with that one. "Maybe he was wearing shoes!" I yelled.

"Shoes can't go through walls," Kaye said.

I started getting very upset. "Fine," I said, "but *something* is wrong with this castle, and I'm going to figure it out."

Beau interrupted with a soothing voice. "Well, we're not going to solve the mystery tonight. Let's get some sleep. We have lessons tomorrow."

I had forgotten about the tutor, but Beau's words reminded me that there were worse things than spooks in the world. I had had enough of this day. I was ready for some dry under-breeches and bed.

# chapter ten

The next morning Kaye woke me by pounding on the bedpost and shouting, "Wake up, sluggard! I think your bed is too close to the fireplace, because you're sleeping like a log!"

I cracked open my eyes and saw the pale, watery light of dawn through the tower window. It was going to be another cloudy day.

"Stop it, Kaye," I muttered. "It's too early for jokes. I'm not ready to get up yet."

"What? You're always the first one up every morning. Are you sick?"

Now that Kaye mentioned it, I noticed my head was pounding, probably from my tumble down the stairs yesterday. But mostly I felt sick at the thought of facing yet another tutor.

"I guess I don't feel too good this morning," I mumbled into my pillow.

"You probably ate too much mutton last night," Kaye said teasingly. "You'll feel better once you get up."

"Later," I said in a low voice.

"Fine, but you don't want to miss the tutor again this morning. I'm meeting Beau before lessons. Come join us in the mews as soon as you get up. Don't stay in bed too long."

I heard Kaye clatter down the stairs. I still didn't want to meet the tutor. Maybe I could go exploring and get lost again.

Then I remembered the spooks.

I rolled over and heaved a big sigh. Spooks or tutors? Which was worse? Maybe the spooks would leave me alone in the daytime. I decided to take a chance and explore the library some more.

Upstairs, I threw all my weight backwards as I opened the gigantic library doors. The shriek of the hinges gave me chills. Maybe Kaye was right. Maybe the noises I thought were spooks yesterday could be explained by perfectly ordinary reasons.

The library looked so much grander in the daylight. I didn't love learning, but I did love books. They were rare and beautiful, and I loved seeing how different scribes decorated the writing with drawings of leaves and flowers as well as animals and monsters and people.

Some of the pictures were painted with silver and gold over vibrant colors that glowed in the room's clear light. I imagined men bent over their work tables, carefully mixing colors and putting them on each page in just the right way to copy the sky's own blue and reds as bright as ripe strawberries shining in the summer grasses.

Peeking out the window, I saw a man with a floppy hat and a heavy-looking bag ride up to the stables, leave his horse, and then enter the castle. He looked like he had been traveling for a few days. Soon afterward, Kaye and Beau came out of the mews. I smiled to myself. They would never find me here.

Digging through the piles of books, I found a small book with gold covers set with blue and green gems. It was too pretty to read, so I didn't bother trying. Instead I hid it behind a bookshelf. Then I found a real treasure, a book of stories about Sir Gregory, the most famous knight in the history of Knox. It had big pictures of him slaying a dragon and climbing

a tower and doing other knightly things. I hid that book too so I could try reading it later.

I was so interested in the books that when a really loud voice said, "Reggie!" it almost scared the skin off of me.

I whirled around and saw Kaye with Beau and a man I guessed was the tutor. He was brown-skinned with a smooth, beardless face. His gleaming bald head had a high dome, like the mind inside it took up more room than a regular person's mind. I put my hand on top of my head. It felt flat, compared to the tutor's head. The lines around the tutor's eyes and mouth looked like he might smile a lot, but he wasn't smiling right now. His deep-set, dark eyes sparkled with interest as he looked around the library.

"What are you doing, Reggie?" Kaye asked.

Before I could answer, Beau said, "You weren't in the tower room, so I guessed you might be here since you talked about it last night."

"Well," I stammered, still shaken from being startled, "I thought the library was where we would have lessons. Isn't this the right kind of place to study?"

"Yes," the tutor said. "Look at these windows! We'll have plenty of light here, and a fine collection of books. Yes, this is the right place for lessons."

He surveyed the room, slowly turning in a circle to take it all in, just as I had done the night before. He caught my eye and nodded with approval.

"An excellent choice, Master Reggie," he said bowing slightly. "I am Tutor Alchir." He wore a robe colored like the setting sun or a fresh apricot, bright against his brown skin.

"Good morrow, Tutor Alchir," I said as politely as I could speak to a tutor.

He bowed again and said, "This room must be cleaned before we can work here."

I groaned inside. I hated cleaning. It was bad enough that we had to clean up pig filth yesterday. Now we had to clean a whole library before we could even start lessons— "We can do it!" I shouted. Cleaning was definitely better than lessons.

"Yes," Alchir said. "We will all clean it. It is said that many hands make hard work easier, but even our eight hands may not be enough. However, we will do our best. How should we start?"

"Picking up books?" Beau asked.

"Where shall we put the books?" Alchir asked him.

"On the shelves," Kaye said with confidence.

"Are the shelves ready for books?" Alchir asked.

This was taking forever. "If we clear a table, we can pile the books on it while some of us clean the shelves," I said.

"Very good, Master Reggie," Alchir said. "I see you are a student of logic. Well done. We will do as you suggest."

The tutor clearly knew nothing about me. I wasn't logical. I believed the castle was full of spooks. I volunteered to clean shelves, starting as far away as possible from Alchir.

Kaye worked near me. At the other end of the library, Beau and Alchir stacked books on a table, singing about a bird who brought the springtime back after a cold winter.

Soon Kaye was close enough to jab me in the arm with his pointy finger. "Ouch!" I cried out.

"Sorry," he said. "I was just checking to see if you were Reggie or a spook. What's wrong? You love to be in the middle of everything, but for the past two days, you're nowhere to be found. You hate to clean, but now you volunteer to do it. And you haven't complained once about being hungry today. Has this castle bewitched you?"

I shrugged. "I don't know. Living in a castle is different than I expected," I said. "I thought I'd be done with tutors and learning."

"Alchir seems to like you," Kaye said.

"He doesn't know me," I said. "Just wait and see how he likes me in a few days."

# chapter eLeven

At the end of my row of shelves, I found a narrow doorway in the wall. "Kaye, look," I whispered. It opened onto a small downward-spiraling staircase inside the wall. "Let's see where it goes," I said.

Kaye laughed and said, "Now you seem more like yourself!"

We crept down the tiny stairs and found a door at the bottom. Kaye peered through the keyhole. "It's empty," he whispered.

We pushed the door open and found ourselves in a richly furnished bedchamber. Painted flowers decorated the walls, including some kinds I had never seen before. I noticed brushes and colors for mixing paint on a table in the nearest corner. Tall candleholders surrounded the table, filled with fat droopy candles, each one marked with the royal seal of Knox. I tiptoed over and saw a small unfinished painting lying flat on the table next to the brushes. It was a painting of a man's face, but it was no one I knew.

Kaye whispered, "Reggie, this is the queen's bedchamber. We should leave."

We slipped into the hallway. As we passed the room where Kaye had been knighted, we heard a man say, "Majesty, conditions are bad in Eldridge. They want their money before the month ends. They're threatening war if they don't get it."

"War! Why?" the queen cried. "No one wants another war. We've worked so hard to keep the peace with Eldridge."

We peered through the open door. The traveling man I had seen in the courtyard earlier held his floppy hat in his hands and looked at the floor as he spoke. "Majesty, I don't think Eldridge really wants another war," he said. "They just want their money. They have problems of their own. From the way things look, Eldridge may end up going to war with itself."

"What does Sir Henry say?" the queen asked.

"He hopes you'll send the money as soon as possible," the man said, reaching into his bag and handing a stack of parchments to the queen. "He wrote to you about it. Is that all, Majesty?"

"Yes, thank you, Grumpet," she said. "You may go."

We flattened ourselves against the wall as Grumpet left. He didn't see us, but when we peeked around the door again, the queen did. She waved us into the room and sat down in a chair with a bump. Her hands shook a little bit as they held the pile of letters on her lap.

She gave us a tired smile. "Did you hear what Grumpet said?"

I nodded. Kaye said, "Is there any money to pay Eldridge?"

"Probably not," the queen said, "but I won't know how much we need until I read these letters."

"Maybe it's not a lot of money," Kaye said. "My father wouldn't ask you to pay the money if you don't have it."

The queen frowned and said, "Your father doesn't know the treasure's missing. In fact, no one knows except us and the knights who were here when the king died. Your father was in Eldridge long before that happened."

"Are you going to tell him it's missing now?" Kaye asked.

"Maybe," the queen said, "but if I do, he'll want to come back here, and I think the king of Eldridge needs his help right now. It sounds like things are bad in Eldridge."

I tapped the queen's arm. "Will there be a war if we don't pay the money?" I asked.

"I don't know," she answered. "Rumor says that Eldridge is about to break into a civil war. It's possible the king might decide that attacking Knox is a good way to make the people of Eldridge forget their differences and stick together."

"Your Majesty," Kaye said, "I'm going to find that treasure for you before the month ends."

"If you find the treasure, I'll be very happy, Kaye, but I'll find a way to pay Eldridge their money somehow. It's not your job to stop this war. It's mine."

"Yes, Your Majesty," Kaye said, sweeping a grand bow and swatting my foot so I would do the same. I bowed, but dropped my bookshelf cleaning rag. I tried to grab it, but lost my balance and had to prop myself up with both hands on the floor.

Queen Vianne laughed out loud, but held her head like the laughing hurt. "Thank you, boys. Now go back to your lessons. Oh, and Kaye," she added, "I'm sure there's a letter for you from your father. I'll give it to you this evening."

"Thank you, Your Majesty," Kaye said, and we left.

On the way back to the library, he said, "Reggie, I have to start looking for the treasure today."

"Do you still have the clue?" I asked. "Let's look at it again. Maybe we missed something last night."

"It's in the tower room," Kaye said, "but we shouldn't bother with it anymore. It's the worst clue I ever saw. I think I should search the entire castle, room by room, until I find the treasure."

In the library, Beau and Alchir sang a new song about broken bones, broken stones, and a broken heart. It sounded gloomy, but they laughed a lot when they made mistakes. They had cleaned the dust off one table and set four chairs around it. Someone had put some parchment and quills in the middle of the table. My stomach hurt when I saw that, but it didn't distract me from what Kaye had just said.

"Searching the castle room by room will take forever," I said. "We don't have that kind of time. We need a place to start, and the terrible clue is all we have."

"*All hope is gone, I am alone,*" Alchir sang in the background.

"It's the best thing I can think of right now," Kaye said. "And anyway, you like to explore, so you can do that while I look for the treasure."

"*My heart's a cold and broken stone,*" Beau and Alchir sang together loudly, finishing the song.

# chapter twelve

My stomach felt even worse—like a giant hand had grabbed my guts and started squeezing. "Kaye," I said, completely shocked, "you don't want me to help you find the treasure?"

Alchir interrupted. "So you are back," he said.

Kaye blushed and said, "We're sorry, Tutor Alchir. We were working in the back and—"

Alchir waved his hand through the air. "No," he said. "I'm not angry because you left. I would only be angry if you hadn't come back. I, too, saw the small staircase and wondered where it led."

Kaye said, "It goes to the queen's rooms. She, um, was not in them this morning."

"Ah," Alchir said, "This was the old king's library. He loved his books so much that I imagine he wanted to be able to get to them easily at any time of night or day." He gazed around the room with a peaceful expression on his face. "This is a most remarkable library. Never have I seen such a collection."

After a moment, he said, "We can continue cleaning tomorrow. Come to the table. I want to see how well you read and write. All of you are far from home, so please write to your families. I will also write a letter to my daughter. She will be joining me here soon."

"Why are you writing to her if she's coming here anyway?" Beau asked.

"So she will know I am thinking of her," Alchir replied. "And like you, she needs to practice reading."

I sat down and stared at the parchment in front of me. I dipped my pen in the ink a few times. I drew a picture of the castle at the bottom of the page. I drew a tree. I drew a dog walking up the tree just like he would walk on the ground. Then I peeked at what the others were doing. All three of them were writing as fast as they could. Word after word piled up on their pages.

I sighed and started writing. *Dear Mum,* I wrote. *The castle is good. I have a tutor. He taught the queen. His head is bald and shiny. Tell Father. He will be glad. Two boys named Tom work in the kitchen. The food is good here. I am well. Love from Reggie.*

I used my best handwriting, but even in real books, I thought letters were ugly—short and crowded, made of lines that looked like dying worms and stubby squirrel tails and broken sticks squashed together and hunched over like old women. All letters looked alike to me.

I wanted to tell my mum about the spook and the missing treasure and the possible war, and how Kaye didn't want my help finding the treasure, but it would have taken too long. Instead, I drew a picture of the falcon carving over the library door, making angry scratches on the page with my pen. Tiny ink dots spattered all over my drawing, giving the falcon freckles like Tom Spot's face.

When I finally looked up, everyone was staring at me.

"Are you finished, Reggie?" Beau asked.

"Almost," I said. "I just have to finish the wing feathers." I added some quick lines to some of the feathers and heard Kaye clear his throat. I looked up again.

"Are you done with your letter?" Kaye asked.

"Oh! Yes, I finished a while ago," I said.

Alchir smiled. "Good. Now that you have practiced writing, I will hear your reading. It's too easy to read your own writing, so give your letters to someone else."

Kaye and Beau changed parchments and then Beau changed again with me. I looked at Kaye's letter. It filled up the whole page. It would take all day to read it.

"Begin, Beau," Alchir said. Beau stared at my letter. Then he moved it closer to his eyes. I didn't know why he didn't just read it. It was nice and short. Then I remembered what I had written about Alchir's bald head. I felt my whole face turning red.

Beau's face was red too. "I'm sorry, I can't read it," he said. I was thankful he didn't embarrass me in front of the tutor.

Kaye took the page and studied it. "Did you write it in code, Reggie?" he asked.

I wrinkled up my forehead. "No," I said. "It's just ordinary. What's wrong with it?"

"I can read it," Kaye said, "but the words are turned inside-out. You've put the middle letters of the words at the beginnings and ends of the words."

"How can you tell?" I asked. "All the letters look like lumps and bumps wherever I put them."

Alchir took my letter and studied it for a moment. Then he laughed out loud. I couldn't take it anymore.

I jumped to my feet and glared at Alchir. "You're just like every other tutor I've ever had. They laugh at me and then leave because I'm stupid. I'm sick of it. This time, I'm leaving first." I ran out of the library as fast as I could.

# chapter thirteen

I ran to the falcon mews because it was the last place anyone would look for me. I didn't care if Oriana decided to peck my eyes out. At least I wouldn't have to see anyone look at me like I was an idiot anymore. It was cool inside the heavy stone building, and I found a small stool to sit on. Oriana preened her feathers and ignored me.

I sat there for a long time with my head on my knees, rolling my bead between my fingers. Someone sat down in the gravel next to me. I waited a while before looking up. I was surprised to see Beau with a parchment in his hand.

"What are you doing here?" I asked.

He laughed. "Me? I'm always here. You're the stranger in the mews."

"Sorry," I said. "Am I in the way?"

"Of course not," Beau said. "I'm glad you're here. Why would you be in the way?"

"I'm always in the way," I said. "Think about it. When Kaye and I rescued you from the bandits, I was stuck in a tree. When Kaye beat Melchor in the tournament, I was chained to a wall. I can't read or write. And now Kaye doesn't even want me to help him find the treasure. Melchor's right. I'm useless. I should go home."

"Don't listen to Melchor," Beau said. "He's a liar. You're not useless."

"Well, why won't Kaye let me help him look for the treasure? We're good at finding things together—or at least we used to be."

Beau shrugged. "Kaye thinks that if he finds the treasure by himself it will prove Melchor wrong about him and Sir Henry."

"Melchor only said all that to make Kaye mad," I said. "All he really wants is for Kaye to go away. I'm more worried about Milo. He's out to get Kaye." I dropped my bead.

"What's this?" Beau asked, picking it up.

"It's a bead I found at a fair. I was supposed to be buying wool with my father, but I did everything wrong and kept making him angry. So I wandered off to look at the minstrels and acrobats and the things for sale. That's when I found the bead in the grass. It was so round and green that finding it made the day better." Talking about my father made me angry. I shoved the bead back into my pocket.

"Ooh, pockets," Beau teased. "Look at you wearing the latest fashions."

"My mum made me some as soon as she learned what pockets were," I said. "She says I need a place to put the things I find. She's always proud of me, even when I can't do anything right—like writing her a letter."

"Most people can't read or write. You're doing well compared to them."

"Not compared to you and Kaye," I said.

Beau shrugged. "Kaye made a lot of mistakes in his letter. He has to fix them before he can leave."

"Kaye made mistakes?" I said. "He tries to be so perfect all the time."

"Well, he doesn't always succeed. And Alchir got mad at me because I wrote my letter to Oriana, so he sent me down here to read it to her since—as he said—I didn't care to communicate with humans anyway."

"Why did you write to a bird?" I asked, confused.

"It seemed stupid to write to my aunt. She's right here anyway."

"Don't you have any other family?"

Beau sighed. "I have a grandmother somewhere in Vinland. My mum died when I was born, and I won't have anything to do with my father."

"I thought your father was dead," I said, surprised.

Beau looked cross. "Well, he is to me. I don't care if I ever see him again. My aunt and you and Kaye are all the family I have, so I hope you don't decide to go home. It's better here now that we're all friends."

"Really?" I said. "I guess I could stay. I want to see what happens with this treasure anyway."

"And the spooks," Beau said.

"Right." I made a face. "Maybe I imagined the spooks. The noises could have been anything. Kaye might be right about that."

"What about the footprints?" Beau asked.

"I can't explain the footprints," I said.

"Well, you'll have to solve that mystery," Beau said, "or else I'll spend my whole life wondering. Come on, Kaye must be done fixing his letter by now. Let's go see if he's found that treasure yet."

# chapter fourteen

We found Kaye under a bed with his backside sticking out.
Heavy red curtains hung around the bed. The crumpled bed
linens looked like someone had just gotten out of the bed, except for the thin covering of dust that turned them gray. More
of the fat candles marked with the royal seal were scattered
around the room. Tall glass bottles and pots of what looked
like medicine littered the top of a table near the bed. A pile of
rags sat in a pail under the table, and they looked like they might
not smell too good.

"Is this the room where the king *died?*" I asked Beau.

Kaye jumped and I heard a thud as his head hit the under-
side of the bed.

"Ouch!" he yelled, crawling out backwards. He sat up and
rubbed his head. "Reggie, you startled me."

"Sorry," I said, not looking directly at him. I turned to Beau.
"Well, is it?"

He nodded.

"Why didn't anyone clean it up? Didn't anyone take care of
the king? No wonder he died," I cried. Then I had a terrible
idea. "Did anyone even bury the king? Maybe it's his spook
that's loose in the castle."

Kaye glared at me. "Reggie, your imagination is running
away with you. Of course they buried the king. There was a big
funeral and everything."

"Well, someone should have cleaned up this room," I said. "It would have been polite to do that for the king, even if he was dead. Did you look in here yet?" I asked Kaye, lifting the lid of a chest at the foot of the bed. Inside were some clean rags and a box holding more fat candles.

"The king wouldn't hide his treasure in a chest at the bottom of his bed. It's the first place anyone would look," Kaye said.

"Well, he didn't hide it under his bed either," I said in an exasperated voice.

"I'm not looking for treasure," Kaye said. "I'm looking for secret compartments in the floor that might *hold* treasure."

"Did you find any?" Beau asked.

"No," Kaye said, "but I'll keep looking."

He tapped the wooden paneling on the walls, listening for hollow noises. He pressed the carvings around the fireplace, hoping to release a hidden panel. He examined every stone of the floor—even the ones Beau and I sat on while we watched him work.

"Kaye, this is boring," I said. "Can't we help?"

Kaye frowned at me. "No, Reggie, I need to do this myself. I have to show everyone I'm not a spy or a traitor."

"Did you try the fireplace?" I asked. "Maybe the king shoved the treasure up the chimney." I was joking, but Kaye stepped carefully into the fireplace and started peering into the black tunnel of the chimney.

I was so bored I fell over sideways onto the floor and accidentally inhaled a healthy lungful of dust, which made me sneeze three times. Beau leaned over and slapped me hard on the back.

"What did you do that for?" I said. "I was sneezing, not choking, you dolt!" I started kicking at Beau, who started kick-

ing back. While we were kicking, Beau banged against the table and knocked two bottles to the floor, where they crashed against the stones and shattered. It was a great noise.

Kaye pulled his head out of the chimney. A black streak of soot across his forehead gave him one thick eyebrow. When he crossed his arms and glared at us, he looked so fierce we laughed. "This isn't a joke," he said. "If the queen can't pay Eldridge, there might be another war."

"So let us help," Beau said. "It's no fun watching you work."

"You can help by cleaning up the mess you made," Kaye said. He looked and sounded a lot like his mum, but I didn't mention it. He probably wouldn't think it was very helpful of me.

"I'll go find a broom," Beau said. He got to his feet and then pulled me up. "I'll find us something to eat too. All this hard work of helping is making me hungry," he whispered so only I could hear him.

I started laughing again, but walked down the hall so I wouldn't annoy Kaye. Turning a corner, I crashed into Tom Spot. He yelled, fell against the wall, and leaned there, panting for breath and pointing at me. He seemed to be trying to say something.

"Tom! What are you doing up here? Are you all right?" I asked.

"Ratfingers! You gave me a fright, Master Reggie! I thought you were a spook."

I laughed. "Tom, what are rat fingers? I've never heard of them in my life. Rats don't even have fingers. They have claws."

He nodded, catching his breath. "You're right, Master Reggie, but I hate rats—they're nasty, smelly things, always stealing good food. The only thing that would make them worse is fingers."

"Fingers?"

"Aye, Master Reggie, think—if rats had fingers, they'd have tiny, cold, grabbing fingers, always reaching for more." He shuddered. "It's the nastiest thing I can think of."

I made a face. "That is nasty," I said. "Why are you up here, Tom? Won't Abelard be looking for you?"

"I need to tell you something. And I wanted to see those spook's footprints you saw. Can you show me?" he asked.

Finally, something to do! "Follow me," I said, leading the way. "What did you want to tell me?"

"Oh, Master Reggie, the spook came down to the kitchen last night while we were all sleeping."

I stared at him. "You saw the spook? What did it look like?" I asked. Then after a moment I added, "You sleep in the kitchen?"

"Aye, us boys do. It's nice and warm down there all the time. But last night, you remember how Master Abelard kept telling Embert to mend his sleeve?"

"Yes," I said, not understanding what that had to do with the spook.

"Before we went to sleep, he told him again, but Embert can't mend, so me and Tom were trying to help him. Only we can't mend either, so Tall Tom said to cut it off and Embert said it was his only shirt and I said to tie it in a knot so it wouldn't fall in the food. We started arguing, and it got loud. Then Master Abelard hollered at us to forget about the sleeve and go to sleep. So we did."

"So?" I asked.

"Well the spook came in the night and sewed up the sleeve!" Tom cried.

"How do you know it was the spook?" I asked. "Did any of you see it?"

"No, we were asleep, but it had to be the spook. You gave us all the creeps with your tale, and Embert was sniveling about the spook after you left. So when Master Abelard hollered at us to go to sleep, he left us the key. We locked every door tight from the inside so we didn't have to fear anyone coming in."

I shook my head. "Locked doors wouldn't stop a spook," I said.

"That's what I said, but no one listened," Tom said. "And that's why it had to be the spook. No one else could have come into the kitchen."

"You're right," I said. "Too bad you didn't see it."

"But there's more, Master Reggie. When the spook mended Embert's sleeve, it left him a treat."

"What was it?" I asked.

"A sweet. A little yellow block with specks. It smelled like honey. Embert was too scared to taste it, but Tall Tom said he wouldn't let a sweet go to waste, so he took it. He's been sucking on it all morning and grinning like a fox. Now he's bragging about how brave he is to eat the spook's sweets. I came up here to see the footprints for myself and show him who's braver."

"You really think the spook left the sweet?" I asked as I started walking again.

"Had to," Tom said. "The doors were locked. And there's something not normal about that sweet. Tom's breath smells like flowers now, not old meat. I wish the spook would leave more sweets for him."

We climbed some stairs and came out in the long paneled corridor where I had made dust angels last night. But the hall in front of us was empty, scoured clean and polished until not even a single fluff of dust remained. It was now the cleanest place in the whole castle.

I grabbed Tom's arm in shock. "Tom, I'm sure this is the place. But last night it was covered in dust. I was on the floor and I got it all over me, did you see me?"

"Aye. You looked like a sheep sheared by a blind man, all wooly-tufty and messy. Maybe this is the wrong place?"

"No, I remember exactly. I know it was this hall. The footprints were right here," I said, walking halfway down the hall and pointing to the ground at my feet. "But now they're gone. What happened?"

"I know," Tom said. "The spook didn't want to be found out, so it came back and cleaned so you wouldn't find its footprints again."

I scratched my head. "Maybe you're right. But it's very strange."

"That's what spooks are, Master Reggie. Strange."

I stared up and down the hallway for so long that Tom finally said, "I have to go back now, Master Reggie. They'll be wondering where I am."

"What? Oh, sorry, Tom," I said. "Thanks for telling me about the sleeve. I'll come down and see it later."

After he left, I lay down on the floor where I had made the dust angel last night. Everything looked exactly the same, but now it was clean. It was the same hallway, I was sure of it. Puzzled, I wandered off to find Kaye and Beau. I hoped Beau had remembered to bring some food. I needed it more than ever now.

# chapter fifteen

I decided to go see about that snack myself, thinking that if I went down to the kitchen, I could investigate Embert's mended sleeve. To my surprise, I found Beau leaning against the table, watching Abelard cut noodles out of dough with quick slashes of his knife. I sniffed the air once and then pulled in a deep breath—something smelled amazing!

"Beau, what are you doing here? I thought you were getting a broom." I turned to the cook and added, "Good morrow, Master Abelard."

"I did," Beau said, pointing to the ground where a broom lay at his feet.

"Good morrow, Master Reggie," Abelard said. I waved at the Toms and Embert.

"Why didn't you bring the broom upstairs?" I asked.

"It's my fault, Master Reggie," Abelard said. "I promised to pack a basket of food for you boys to eat while you explore, but the meat pies are just finishing and His Grace said he would wait because he thought you would want him to."

I grinned. "Well, I do like meat pies. Good idea, Beau."

I watched Tall Tom carefully remove some piping hot meat pies from the oven. The rich juices bubbled out from under the golden crusts and filled the air with all my favorite smells. I knew most people liked their meat pies cold, but I liked mine any way I could get them.

Tom Spot waved me over to where he and Embert were putting wood on the fire.

"Show him, Embert," Tom Spot said.

Embert held out his arm. The dangling flap I remembered from yesterday was neatly reattached to the rest of the sleeve with careful stitches.

"It's a wonder," I said. I looked at Embert. "You didn't feel anything?"

He shook his head with wide eyes and one finger in his mouth. Then he pulled down on my arm until he could whisper in my ear. I could barely hear his wavering voice as he asked, "Am I going to die, Master Reggie?" He put his finger back in his mouth.

"What?" I cried. "Why would you think that?"

Tom Spot sighed. "He's afraid he's going to die because the spook touched him. He's been worrying about it all day. I told him he'd be fine."

I knelt on the floor and put my hand on Embert's shoulder. "The spook didn't hurt you last night, right?"

Embert shook his head.

"Maybe this spook isn't so bad," I said. "It helped you. I think it's your friend."

Embert pulled his chin in and leaned backward, looking at me carefully to see if I was joking. Then he gave me a smile almost as big as Beau's and threw his arms around my neck. I let him. He wasn't very old—maybe about six. I wondered who his mother and father were and if they missed him.

"There now, Embert," Abelard called from across the kitchen. "Don't be hanging on the young master. It's not your place."

He let go and I patted him on the head. "You're a good boy, Embert. No wonder the spook likes you best."

Tall Tom's shoulders slumped when I said this and I heard Tom Spot behind me trying not to laugh. "What's so funny?" I whispered to him.

"Tall Tom," he said. "You put him in his place. All morning he's been bragging about how brave he is, but now that you said Embert's the spook's favorite, Tom's got nothing to brag about!"

Abelard handed a heavy basket to Beau. "Take the broom, Reggie, and we'll go eat with Kaye," Beau said.

I grabbed the broom and thanked Abelard as we left the kitchen. When we reached the passage that led to the old king's room, I saw Sir Milo walking away from us.

"What's *he* doing here?" I asked Beau, feeling afraid. I ran to the king's room and found Kaye on the floor in the middle of the broken bottles. His pink palms slowly turned red as blood oozed around bits of glass stuck in his skin. One eye was red and puffy. The front of his clothes sparkled with speckles of glass and his hurt eye shone with tears.

I dropped the broom with a clatter. "What happened?" I cried.

"Milo 'accidentally' tripped me and I fell in the glass," Kaye said in a dry, raspy voice. "I hit my eye on the table on the way down."

"You must be hurt pretty bad," Beau said. "You're crying."

I knew better than that. Kaye only cried when he was too furious to speak. Milo must have said something really mean to him.

"What did Milo say?" I asked.

Kaye shrugged. "More lies. I'm a spy. My father is a traitor. Now he's making the king of Eldridge demand money from the queen because he knows Knox can't pay and it will cause a war."

Beau set the food basket on the chest at the foot of the bed and examined Kaye's injuries. "This looks bad," he said. "Come down to the courtyard and we'll take care of your hands."

With a sad sniff in the direction of the abandoned meat pies, I followed after them.

In the courtyard, Beau drew a bucket of water from the well and poured it gently over Kaye's hands. Blood and glass washed to the ground. After looking closely at the wounds, Beau said, "The cuts aren't deep, but I'm going to get Nicolette to patch you up. Reggie, see if there's any glass left in his hands that you can pull out."

I eased one or two pieces of glass out of Kaye's hand. "I don't see any more. Does it hurt?"

"Yes." He heaved a sigh. "This is really taking up my treasure-hunting time."

"Are you joking?" I asked. "You just got beat up by a huge knight and you're worried about wasting time? What's wrong with you?"

"What's wrong with me?" Kaye said, turning red again. The blood seeped out of his cuts a little faster. "I'll tell you what's wrong. This wouldn't have happened if you and Beau weren't messing around. You didn't even clean up the glass. All morning you wanted to help, but you only made my work harder. It's your fault this happened."

"What?" I said. "Milo tripped you. Not me."

"You broke the glass."

"Beau broke the bottles."

"Because you were kicking him!"

"Kaye, I'm really sorry you got hurt, but Milo did it. I'm afraid he'll hurt you worse next time. I think you should go home where it's safe."

"NO!" Kaye yelled. "I have to find the treasure so there won't be another war. Don't you know this is important? All you do is stand around wasting time while I search."

"You won't let me help!" I said.

"Well, where were you when I got hurt?" Kaye asked. "Doing nothing, as usual," he said in a nasty voice.

I couldn't take it anymore. I turned around and left him alone with his wounds.

# Chapter Sixteen

I ran to the library, and as soon as I entered, I felt calmer. Maybe it was the light streaming through the big windows or the smell of books, but I felt at home here. I really wanted to talk to my mum. She always helped me feel better.

Then I remembered the pens and parchment Alchir had left on the table. I could write to my mum and tell her everything. I pulled a sheet of parchment from the stack and chose a pen.

I wrote, *Dear Mum, the castle is not good. Kaye is mad at me.*

I stopped writing. I had so many thoughts in my head that I felt like they were pushing against the backs of my eyeballs, but I couldn't write fast enough to keep up with those thoughts. Then I realized I couldn't write about anything without explaining something else first. It would take forever. Finally I crushed the parchment into a ball and hurled it across the room, yelling, "I'll *never* be able to write what I want!"

As I threw the parchment, it sprang open and flopped to the ground in front of me. Frustrated, I kicked it around the library and stomped on it and threw it again. It landed on a table coated with dust near the back of the library. I left it there. I hated it so much.

I took the book about Sir Gregory out of its hiding place and settled down on a bench under one of the big windows. I saw Nicolette in the courtyard helping Kaye, rubbing herbs and ointments onto his cuts and bruises.

The writing in my book was too hard to read, so I studied the pictures instead, sliding my green bead along the smooth pages. My favorite painting showed Sir Gregory creeping into a sleeping dragon's lair and stealing its treasure. I smiled, imagining the dragon's surprise when it woke up!

I leaned back and daydreamed about being brave Sir Gregory and stealing a dragon's treasure. It was fun to imagine, but I knew it wasn't the life for me. I would worry too much.

Glancing into the courtyard again, I saw Nicolette bandaging Kaye's hands and knees. I sighed and looked at the dragon picture again. Suddenly I realized that the dragon had a *lot* of treasure. There was no way Sir Gregory could have carried it away all by himself. He must have had help, and if Sir Gregory could have help, then surely Kaye could too. Of course, Kaye would never agree, so I'd have to find a way to help him secretly.

As I put the book away, I thought I heard a faint scraping sound coming from the back of the library, but I didn't see anything unusual.

I forgot about it when I noticed a very thin book crammed between some thick, heavy books on a shelf. I liked the idea of a short book and hoped it was something I could read, so I pulled it off the shelf and opened it.

Whoever wrote this book had worse handwriting than I did. I couldn't read it, even though it looked familiar. I was about to put it back when I saw that it was full of scratchy drawings that reminded me of Oriana. I rolled my eyes. I could draw better than this! Who made this book?

I flipped to the first page. It said, "My Falcons" and underneath that it said King F——. I couldn't read the last word, but I guessed it meant King Frederic, which was the old king's name.

I didn't like the book. I couldn't read it and the pictures were terrible, but I stuck it in my book hiding place to show Beau later. He loved falcons as much as the old king had and might like to see the book.

Just then, my stomach roared at me. I wondered if I could sneak down to the kitchen and get something to eat. Then I remembered the basket we had left in the old king's room. A basket of meat pies! I couldn't wait to sink my teeth into one.

I ran over to grab my stupid letter, but when I reached the table, I couldn't believe what I saw. My letter lay on the table where I had flung it. A little yellow block rested on a cloth next to it. And in the dust all around it, someone had drawn a big heart.

The spook had struck again, but this was not what I expected from a spook.

"Spook sweets," I whispered, examining the yellow block. It was hard and sticky and smelled like flowers, just as Tom Spot had said. Maybe Embert wasn't the spook's only favorite! I wrapped the sweet in the cloth, putting it in my pocket with the letter. I looked around the empty room and called out, "Thank you, Friend," before dashing out of the room as fast as possible. The spook seemed friendly, but I wasn't taking any chances.

I ran all the way to the old king's room, and stopped in the doorway like I had crashed into an invisible wall. Kaye was there, sweeping up the glass with the broom. He had stripped the linen off the bed, made it into a bundle, and set it on the wooden chest next to the food basket.

"What are you doing?" I asked.

He shrugged. "You're right. It's sad no one ever cleaned this room after the king died. Nicolette said if I brought her the bed linen, she'd send it to the village washerwomen."

I looked at the bandages on Kaye's hands. "Here, give me the broom," I said. "That must hurt your hands." I swept the glass into a pile and pulled my letter out of my pocket. I flattened it on the floor and tried to sweep the glass onto the parchment. "Why aren't you hunting for treasure right now?" I asked. "Aren't you afraid of wasting time?"

Kaye bent down to hold the paper flat against the floor. "Nicolette says I need to rest."

"You're not resting," I said.

"I was looking for you. I thought you'd come for the meat pies sooner or later."

"Why were you looking for me?" I asked, a little rudely.

He squatted on the floor and squinted at the parchment. I forgot he could read my bad handwriting. He looked up at me. "I'm not mad at you. I'm sorry I was mean. I was worried. I know the queen says it's not my job to stop the war, but if there *is* a war, my father's going to have to fight in it. He could die," he finished in a whisper.

I hadn't thought of that. I felt terrible. Crouched on the floor, Kaye looked smaller than Embert.

He kept talking. "I know my father's been gone a long time, but at least I can still hope that he'll come back someday."

I swept the glass onto the parchment and then Kaye folded it into a pouch.

I didn't know what to say. "Are you hungry?" I finally said.

Kaye nodded and stood up.

"Me too," I said. I put the bundle of linen on the floor by the door and we sat on the chest and helped ourselves to some meat pies. After a few bites, I said, "Your father will come back. I know it."

"Thanks," Kaye said.

After we ate, we spent the afternoon with Beau and Oriana. I stayed away from Oriana, but I had to admit she was incredible. Watching her soar and drop and glide was impressive, and Kaye cheered up again once he and Oriana caught a rabbit together.

Kaye had always liked chasing rabbits, but he had never caught one until today. If he could accept help from a bird, he could accept help from me. The first thing I needed to do was to take another look at the clue.

# chapter seventeen

I put my plan into action that evening after dinner. Abelard had created a delicious dish out of Kaye's rabbits, preparing them with a sweet and sour spiced sauce. I ate two helpings of that and lots of other food. I even tried a dish of creamed eels for the first time. Then all of us—Queen Vianne, Nicolette, Beau, Kaye, and me—gathered around the fire in the room where Kaye had been knighted.

Kaye and I lay on some soft bearskins near the fire. The queen and Nicolette played chess. I told everyone the story about Sir Gregory sneaking into the dragon's lair and stealing its treasure while it slept. Beau laughed out loud at that one. I thought I heard soft laughter echoing from the walls, but maybe I just imagined it.

"You tell a good story, Reggie," Beau said.

"Thanks," I said.

Kaye asked the queen, "Your Majesty, were there any letters for me from my father this morning?"

"No, Kaye, I'm sorry," the queen said.

Kaye's face fell. "That's strange," he said. "He always writes. I hope he's all right."

"I'm sure he's fine, Kaye," the queen said. "He was probably busy writing letters to me about this money we owe Eldridge."

Kaye nodded. Beau picked up his lute and plucked softly at its strings, because the queen still complained of head pains.

One of the notes jangled against the others, so Beau tuned the instrument until all the notes rang out sweetly. The queen sat close to the fire, but I saw her shiver, so I brought her a cloak.

"Thank you, Reggie," she said, curling up in her chair and tucking the cloak around her feet. "This summer is so cold that I can't ever seem to warm my feet. I miss the sun in Vinland."

"Maybe I can help," Kaye said. He pulled some wool and knitting sticks out of the pouch he wore at his waist. Soon he was knitting something that looked like a stocking. He would be busy for a while. Now was my chance to look at the clue again.

I jumped up. "I'll be right back," I said.

"What's wrong, Reggie?" Nicolette asked.

"Um, nothing," I said. "I just have to go, um, somewhere."

Beau laughed again. "Too much creamed eel, Reggie. I told you you'd be sorry if you ate so much." Everyone laughed, and I slipped out of the room while they were distracted.

Back in the tower room, I opened up the wardrobe. I was sure Kaye had hidden the clue inside. There weren't many places to hide things in the room. It was big, but it was empty. So was the wardrobe.

That left the fireplace and the bed. I started with the bed, lifting the linen and feeling through the mattress. Sure enough, I felt a box inside the straw stuffing. In a moment, I had the parchment in my hand. I unfolded it carefully.

It looked familiar to me—and not because I had seen it last night. The handwriting matched the king's handwriting in the little book I had found in the library. This was no surprise, but now that I had seen the king's awful attempts to sketch his favorite falcons in that same book, I realized something. The scribble on the clue was meant to be a falcon!

It didn't look like a falcon, but it looked enough like the king's terrible drawings that I knew what it was supposed to be. I thought there was something funny about the falcon's eyes, but it was impossible to tell.

A falcon! Now we had somewhere to start. I ran back to the others, hoping I could help Kaye realize for himself that the clue was a falcon.

Kaye was still knitting. He had made two small short stockings and was working on what looked like two more big stockings. Someone had gotten him some more wool—some of it was spun into yarn and the rest was fluffy. The queen was talking to Kaye and the others.

"I'm meeting with the knights tomorrow morning," she said. "Maybe together we can find a way to pay the debt."

"Don't worry, Aunt," Beau said. "Something will turn up. Maybe Kaye will find the treasure."

"That would be wonderful," she said, "but we need another plan in case the lost treasure is just a story."

"Why do we owe Eldridge money anyway?" Beau asked.

The queen frowned. "Well," she said, "you must know something about the war between Knox and Eldridge?"

"It happened the year I was born," Beau said.

Queen Vianne sighed. "Yes. That's when my poor sister—your mother—died."

"My father was knighted then," Kaye said, now knitting the second large stocking.

"That's right," Queen Vianne said. "Your father thought of the plan that ended the fighting."

"What was it?" I asked.

"Have you heard of Abegnayle?" she asked us.

We nodded. Abegnayle was a tiny place in the mountains between Knox and Eldridge. It didn't belong to either country. The stony ground couldn't grow much food, so only a few score of people and their goats lived there. Except for one steep, twisting path that led down to Knox, Abegnayle was cut off from the rest of the world by jagged mountain peaks.

The queen said, "The war between Knox and Eldridge was fought over Abegnayle."

"Why?" Kaye asked. "Nobody wants Abegnayle. There's nothing there but goats and rocks."

The queen shrugged. "It was a foolish war, fought for a foolish reason, but sometimes that is the way with wars. Neither country really wanted Abegnayle, but one day King Frederic decided to make Abegnayle part of Knox. When the people of Eldridge found out, they decided they wanted Abegnayle for themselves. They were willing to fight for it, and so the war began."

"How did Sir Henry end the war?" Beau asked.

"He suggested that King Frederic simply buy Abegnayle from Eldridge."

"But it didn't belong to Eldridge," I said with a frown.

"That's true," the queen said, "but that's why it was such a good idea. It was more than fair to Eldridge, and they knew it, so they agreed that Abegnayle could be part of Knox and that ended the war."

"That's why we owe Eldridge money?" Kaye asked. "We're still paying for Abegnayle?"

"Yes," the queen said, "Knox promised to pay Eldridge a small amount of money each year until Abegnayle was completely paid for. However, this year the king of Eldridge wants all the remaining money at once."

"Why?" I asked.

"Some of the king's subjects are making trouble in Eldridge. They say that Eldridge still owns Abegnayle since Knox never finished paying for it. They want another war with Knox to protect what they think belongs to them. The king believes that if Knox finishes paying for Abegnayle now, he can prevent another war."

"So there really could be a war," Beau said thoughtfully.

"It seems that way," the queen sighed.

Kaye held out his finished invention to the queen. It was a small stocking, stuffed inside of a large stocking. He had filled the space between them with fluffy unspun wool and knitted the tops of the two stockings together so the soft wool wouldn't fall out.

"They look like boots," I said.

The queen slid her feet into the soft boots, "They feel like cushioned stockings. Thank you, Kaye," she said. "They're so nice and warm."

"They're boot-stockings," Beau said. "That's clever, Kaye. You could be rich if you made a lot of those and sold them at a fair."

Kaye shook his head, "No, thank you, Beau. Don't forget, I have a treasure to find."

"You'll find it," I said. He didn't know that we finally had a real clue, but he would soon, if I managed things the right way.

# chapter eighteen

The queen met with her knights the next morning. I wasn't invited, but I snuck into the room anyway. Sir Griswald let me hide behind his chair.

The queen began the meeting by discussing Sir Dworfurd, who was locked in the tower for burning the old king's papers. Today she took away Sir Dworfurd's lands and announced that he was no longer a knight of Knox.

I whispered to Sir Griswald, "I didn't know a knight could be un-knighted."

Sir Griswald nodded. "Aye. It's a terrible punishment and brings shame to the knight and his family. But that Sir Dworfurd didn't have any family here. He wasn't from Knox. He came down from Abegnayle in the mountains."

Surprised to hear about Abegnayle again, I asked, "Why?"

"Abegnayle's a poor, stony place and hard to get to," Sir Griswald said. "If anyone from Abegnayle wants to make something of himself, he comes down to Knox or Eldridge, like Dworfurd did. He did well for himself. Only three men from Abegnayle were ever knighted in Knox."

"Who are the other two?"

Sir Griswald looked around, "Oh, they're gone now. One died of a cough a few months ago. The other one ran away. He thought the castle was haunted and the spooks were out to get him. And now Dworfurd's locked in the tower." He squinted at me. "It was your tutor that caught him burning the papers. Did you know that?"

That was interesting. I wanted to ask another question, but Queen Vianne spoke again. Gesturing toward Kaye's black eye and bandaged hands, she told the knights that although they did not have to like Sir Kaye, she required that they did not hurt him.

"Furthermore," she added, "if I hear that *any* of you have harmed Kaye in any way, I will take away your lands, just as I did to Sir Dworfurd."

The knights muttered, but fell silent as the queen began talking about the money Knox owed Eldridge. "We have no money in the treasury," she said. "Does anyone have any ideas about how we can pay the debt and avoid a war?"

One of the knights asked, "Are you sure the King of Eldridge will declare war on Knox if we don't pay him?"

The queen nodded. "Sir Henry told me this is true."

Another knight laughed meanly and said, "Why doesn't Sir Henry tell the king that we have no money?"

"Sir Henry doesn't know," the queen answered. "No one knew the money was gone until after King Frederic died. So once again, I ask you—does anyone know how we can pay Eldridge?"

A few knights yawned. Others scratched their beards thoughtfully, but no one said anything.

Kaye jumped to his feet. "Your Majesty," he said, "I will keep searching for the missing treasure. Maybe I can find it in time."

The knights burst out laughing. Even Sir Griswald smiled a bit.

Milo called out, "Brat! How could you find it when none of us could?"

"Maybe Sir Runt is small enough to creep into the castle mouse holes and search for treasure there!" another one said.

Sir Melchor rose to his feet and paced to the front of the room. "I see our young friend is just like his father—both of them like to be the center of attention."

Kaye blushed and sat down. Melchor kept talking. "Everyone praises Sir Henry for his valuable service to Knox. But where is Sir Henry? Is he here to help and advise his queen in her time of need? No! He's in Eldridge, encouraging the king to make demands that will bring war. All of this makes me wonder—is Sir Henry really a true friend to Knox?"

"Melchor," the queen said, "I trust Sir Henry. If you have nothing helpful to say, please sit down."

Melchor bowed to the queen. "I can solve our problem."

"Then speak."

"People call Sir Henry Knox's greatest hero. They look to him for answers," Melchor said. "But what kind of hero can a man be to a country he never visits? How loyal can he be to a queen he hasn't met?" Melchor gestured toward Kaye. "How proud a father can he be when he never sees his family?"

Milo laughed. Kaye flushed bright red and glared at Melchor.

"Enough, Melchor," the queen said. "Sit down."

He bowed again toward the queen. "My point, Your Majesty, is that you can look to loyal people who actually live in Knox to help you stop this dangerous and expensive war."

The queen looked annoyed. "Are you talking about yourself, Melchor? If so, please tell me how you wish to help."

Melchor smiled, "Your Majesty always has the interests of her people at heart. I wish to make a gift to Knox. I will pay the debt out of my own money and save the land from war."

The queen looked shocked. Kaye's mouth fell open. Melchor grinned, enjoying the sensation he had caused.

"That would be a noble gift, Sir Melchor," the queen said, "but with no money in the treasury, I could never repay you for such a generous loan."

Melchor beamed. "I said I would make a gift to Knox. There is no need to repay me. It is enough to know that I am helping the people of Knox. However, if you wish to thank me, I would be happy to take Sir Dworfurd's lands. You'll need someone new to look after them and the people who live there."

"True," the queen said. She nodded at Beau. "I had planned to grant Dworfurd's lands to His Grace the Duke, but perhaps I can find something else for him." She looked at Melchor and added, "Or for you. Would you like a gift of land closer to your existing lands? If I recall, Sir Dworfurd's land is near the mountain forests. The ground is stony and the crops poor."

"I love the mountains," Melchor said. "Some of my happiest days as a child were spent near the mountains. I would like to see them again."

He sounded innocent, but he looked sly. I didn't know why Melchor wanted Dworfurd's stony mountain land, but I was pretty sure it wasn't because he liked the scenery. I could tell Kaye was suspicious too.

"Very well," the queen said.

"Don't trust him, Your Majesty!" Kaye called out. "He's hiding something."

"Keep quiet, boy. Show some respect," Melchor growled. Milo grinned with delight.

"Kaye, sit down," Queen Vianne said, frowning. "Melchor has offered to save Knox from a war at great personal cost. He deserves our thanks."

"Your Majesty, trust me to find that treasure!" Kaye said.

Melchor snorted and narrowed his eyes as he advanced on Kaye. "Treasure! You'll never find it. It's not here. It's no secret that the treasure disappeared at the same time that Sir Henry left Knox. Perhaps he took it with him."

Kaye squeezed his hands into tight fists at his sides. "My father's no thief!"

"He's the worst kind of thief!" Melchor said. "He pretends to be loyal and helpful, but he stole Knox's treasure and now he plots with Eldridge to steal Knox's throne."

"Peace, Melchor," the queen said. "I will accept your generous offer to pay the debt and we will have no more talk of war or treason."

Kaye looked like he wanted to bite Melchor. Words exploded out of his mouth. "You're jealous!" he cried. "You're jealous because my father's more important than you. You want to buy the same kind of honor he's earned and you lie to make yourself look better than him!"

"You tell lies yourself!" Melchor roared, turning purple in the face. "You say you can find that treasure and save the kingdom, but no one can find it."

"I will find it!" Kaye cried. "Then the queen won't need to touch your dirty money." Milo leaped up with a murderous glint in his eye, but some other knights pushed him back into his seat and made him stay there.

Melchor crossed his arms and turned to the queen. "I changed my mind, Your Majesty."

The queen turned pale, but she kept calm and said, "Do you no longer wish to help Knox avoid a war?"

"I will still provide the money," Melchor said, "but only if you agree that on the day you give my money to Eldridge, you will also send a proclamation throughout the kingdom declaring that this boy here," he pointed at Kaye, his finger shaking with anger, "this unspeakable brat...this embarrassment to Knox... is no longer a knight of Knox and shall never be one again."

The queen frowned. "What if Kaye finds the treasure first?"

Melchor laughed. "He won't. But if he does, you certainly won't need my money to pay the debt."

"That's a very serious demand, Sir Melchor," the queen said. "What do you think, Sir Kaye?"

Kaye looked at the queen with big eyes and swallowed once or twice. All his anger gone, he answered in a small voice, "I agree to Melchor's demands. If I can't find the treasure, you will still need his help to avoid a war."

Melchor's smug smile made me want to punch him.

The queen sighed. "I thank you both for your willingness to help Knox. Sir Melchor, since this is a matter of great importance, I think it would be best to write it down so we can all agree on the terms, don't you?"

Melchor blinked with surprise, but said in a hearty voice, "Yes, of course, by all means, what an excellent idea. Let's have it written down."

The queen sent for her chancellor and gave him instructions in a low voice. Sitting down at a table, he quickly wrote a long page of words and brought it back to the queen.

After reading the document, the queen told the knights, "This says that Melchor agrees to pay the money Knox owes to Eldridge. On the day that this happens, Sir Kaye will no longer be a knight of Knox. He will also lose any chance to ever become a knight of Knox in the future. These things will happen unless Sir Kaye finds the missing treasure before the day the king of

Eldridge demands his money." The queen looked around the room. "Does everyone understand?"

The knights nodded. Some of them were grinning, but Sir Griswald whispered to me, "Ach, it's hard on the boy. He's a brave lad, but stubborn too—just like his father."

The queen handed the parchment to Sir Melchor. "Please look this over, Sir Melchor, and be sure that you agree with it."

Melchor looked carefully at the parchment, line by line. I didn't like him, but I felt sorry for anyone who had to read that long, awful page.

"It is acceptable, Your Majesty," Melchor said grandly, making a fancy bow to the queen.

"Will you affix your seal to the page to show that you accept the terms?" the queen asked.

"Yes, yes, certainly," Melchor said. The chancellor brought wax and string and Melchor pressed his ring into the hot wax. The queen did the same with the royal seal and returned the parchment to the chancellor.

She stood up. "I thank you, my knights, for the help you give to the people of Knox. We are finished here, please return to your duties." The queen left the room, and the knights soon followed.

Kaye stood alone in the middle of the room, looking lost.

# CHAPTER NINETEEN

"Kaye, are you all right? Your face looks green," Beau said.

Kaye shook his head like a dog shakes water off its coat. He drew a few deep breaths. Then he covered his face with his bandaged hands and groaned. "Why didn't I keep quiet? I could have searched for the treasure secretly and even if I didn't find it, Melchor would have paid the debt and I'd still be a knight."

"We told you to be careful with Melchor," I said. "He knows exactly how to make you mad enough to do something stupid."

One of Kaye's eyeballs glared at me through his fingers.

"Reggie, that's not helpful," Beau said sternly.

"Sorry," I said, "but this is awful. I can't believe the queen did that to you! I thought she was your friend."

Kaye dropped his hands and said, "The good of the kingdom comes first, Reggie. If I had listened to you, I wouldn't be in this mess, but I couldn't let him call my father a thief. I thought that if I found the treasure, no one could say my father stole it."

"There's still time," I said.

"How long?" Kaye asked.

"The messengers from Eldridge will come to collect their money in two weeks," Beau said.

Kaye's shoulders drooped. "That's not enough time to search the entire castle."

I thought for a minute. Two weeks wasn't enough time to help Kaye figure out the falcon clue by himself. I had to tell him.

"I know something," I said, "but promise me you won't be angry with me."

"Kaye can't waste time being angry," Beau said. "If he does, he may never be a knight again."

Kaye nodded. "What do you know, Reggie?"

"I looked at the clue again."

"But I hid it!" Kaye said, sounding angry already.

"I found it," I said. "It's not a big room, Kaye. There were only three places you could have hidden it."

"Calm down, Kaye," Beau said. "What did you find, Reggie?"

"The terrible clue," I said. "It's a drawing of a bird—a falcon."

They looked doubtful. "Are you sure?" Beau asked. "It didn't look like much of a falcon to me."

"I know it's a falcon. I promise. And there's something funny about its eyes."

"Falcons don't have funny eyes. They have excellent eyes," Beau said. "That's why they're such good hunters."

"That's what I saw," I said.

"I guess it's a place to start," Kaye said, "but there are falcons everywhere. Look." He pointed at the fireplace mantle. There were falcons carved across the entire front of it.

"It's going to take a while to look at all the falcons in the castle," Beau said. "Where should we start? In here? Or maybe in the gallery?"

"You should start with your lessons," Alchir's voice said. He was standing in the doorway. "I've been waiting for you for a while now."

We looked at each other. None of us wanted to go with him, but Beau shrugged and whispered, "There are falcons in the library too." So we went.

I trailed far behind the others. Until now, I had forgotten about shouting at Alchir and running away yesterday, but I had a feeling that Alchir remembered perfectly.

By the time I got to the library, Kaye and Beau were hard at work. Suddenly, Alchir stood next to me. I was so embarrassed I didn't know where to look. My face felt hot.

"Good morrow, Master Reggie," Alchir said.

"Good morrow, Tutor Alchir. I'm sorry I yelled at you and ran away yesterday." Alchir didn't say anything. This made me mad. I looked him straight in the face and said, "You shouldn't have laughed at me. I can't help being unteachable. I try to learn. I try really hard." I couldn't look at him anymore, so I looked at the dust on the floor and said, "I always do everything wrong."

Alchir frowned. "Who said you were unteachable?"

"Other tutors. I've had lots of them, one after another. They laugh because I'm stupid. They tell my father I'm unteachable. Then they leave and he gets angry at me, because he pays the tutors a lot of money and I never learn anything."

"I see. I shouldn't have laughed yesterday, but I didn't understand your trouble. I wasn't laughing at you. Your letter was funny."

I blinked. "It was?"

"Yes. I liked it. I wanted to read more," Alchir said. "Do you have more you want to write?"

I blushed. "I can't. It takes too long. Talking is easier."

"Today you will talk and I will write what you say."

"Really? I have a lot to say," I said.

"Good. Come with me; we will sit away from the others so we do not disturb them."

"What are they doing?" I asked.

"A language lesson—Latin," he said, leading me to the back of the library. We passed the dusty table where I had found the sweet inside the heart yesterday.

The heart had been brushed away, but I saw something new next to it. I stared at it and yelled, "Kaye! Look at this!"

Kaye and Beau came running over. "What is it?" Kaye asked.

"There's a drawing in the dust on the table," I said. "It's a clue."

"Is it a bird?" Beau asked.

"Not just any bird," I said. "It's a falcon and an arrow pointing that way!" I pointed toward the library door.

Kaye folded his arms. "Reggie, did you draw this?"

"Of course not! Why would you ask that?"

"If you didn't draw it, who did?" Kaye asked.

"Oh," I said. "It was the spook. It's friendly—at least to me and Embert."

"A spook?" Alchir asked with raised eyebrows.

I glanced at him and said, "I told you I had a lot to write."

Kaye rolled his eyes. "You know there are no such things as spooks," he said.

"Then who drew this clue in the dust?" I asked. "It wasn't me. I just got here. No one knows we're looking for a falcon, so who else could have drawn this but the spook? In fact, the spook left me a sweet on this very table yesterday and mended Embert's sleeve."

Kaye sighed and said, "Reggie, spooks don't leave sweets and do mending. Did you ever think your spook might be a person?"

"Then that person can walk through walls!" I shouted.

Beau stepped between us and said, "Let's just see what this drawing means. Whoever made it seems to be trying to help."

"Fine," Kaye said.

We followed the arrow. I saw several falcon carvings, but I went straight to the big one over the door. While Beau and Kaye examined the other falcons, I carefully climbed the library shelves next to the door until I could reach the carving. As soon as I was high enough, I could see that its eyes were made of shiny black stones set into the wood. One of them was missing.

"It's missing an eye!" I cried out. "This must be the one the king drew on the clue. I knew there was something wrong with its eyes."

I touched the dusty carving gently. The head was crooked. I gave it a little twist and a pull like yanking a stopper out of a bottle and it popped into my hand.

I stuck my fingers into the hollow bird and pulled out a folded piece of parchment. I handed it to Kaye, made sure the bird was empty, stuck its head back on, and climbed down.

We crowded around Kaye to see what the note said. There were only two words written in the king's shaky handwriting, and I couldn't read them at all.

Kaye squinted hard at the words. "Sagitta tacita," he read aloud. "Is that Latin?" he asked Alchir.

"Yes. It means silent arrow," Alchir said.

"Silent arrow," Beau said slowly, as if he was thinking out loud. "Arrows are mostly silent—at least until they hit the target."

I nodded, remembering our journey to the castle and the noise the arrow made when it hit the tree.

"That means it would have to be an especially silent arrow for the king to call it that," Kaye said.

"Where would we find arrows?" I asked.

"Maybe in the armory, where the weapons are kept," Beau said, before turning to Alchir. "Can we go look in the armory right now?"

"I'm sorry," Alchir said. "I promised the queen that you will do lessons until midday each day. But soon I must go meet my daughter, and for the last part of her journey we will travel here together. There will be no lessons while I am gone."

Kaye climbed the shelves and put the parchment back inside the falcon. The four of us returned to our work and waited for midday to finally arrive.

# chapter twenty

That afternoon we found plenty of arrows in the armory, but not one of them seemed any more silent than the others. Then Beau had a great idea. He said that since we had already found one clue inside a carving, we should look for the silent arrow in some other kind of artwork. After all, what was more silent than a statue or a painting?

We spent a few afternoons inspecting all the art in the castle, but even the long gallery outside the library disappointed us. All the art showed people holding swords—never arrows.

Beau fell to the ground next to a suit of armor holding up yet another sword. Closing his eyes, he said, "I can't believe there isn't a single arrow in any of the art in this castle."

I couldn't help laughing. "It looks like that suit of armor just knocked you down with its sword," I said.

"I feel like I've been knocked down," he said. "I thought I had such a good idea, but it was all wrong."

I sat down next to him. "You had a great idea," I said. "It was worth trying."

Beau looked more cheerful, but Kaye stood over us with folded arms and said, "I don't think we should use the clues anymore. It's taking too long. The messengers from Eldridge will be here in about a week and a half. We should go back to searching the castle room by room while we still have time."

"What about the silent arrow?" Beau asked.

Kaye shrugged. "I'm not sure that's even a real clue."

"But you were there when we found it!" I cried.

"How did we find it?" Kaye asked.

"We were looking for a falcon, and we found one drawn on the library table with an arrow pointing to the carving where the clue was hidden."

Kaye raised an eyebrow and asked, "Who drew the arrow on the table?"

I blushed. "The spook," I whispered.

"There's no such thing as a spook," he said, shaking his head. "I'll tell you what I think really happened."

"What?" Beau asked. I couldn't say a word.

"I think Melchor overheard our conversation after the meeting of the knights. He learned we were looking for a falcon. When Alchir came to get us he went to the library, drew in the dust, and hid a false clue in the carving."

"How would he know that the carving is hollow?" I asked. "And does Melchor even know Latin? That doesn't make sense."

"It makes more sense than a spook," Kaye said. "And Melchor wants to make sure that I don't find the treasure. What better way could he do that than to waste my time with false clues?"

"Maybe you're right," Beau said.

"Yes, but—" I stopped talking. Deep inside, I knew the clues were important, but I was always wrong about everything. If Kaye and Beau wanted to search the castle room by room, I might as well help them out.

"Fine," I said in a tired voice. "Where do we start?"

Kaye began walking around the edges of the big room, knocking on the wood paneling.

"What are you doing?" I asked.

"Listening for hollow sounds," Kaye said.

"Those walls behind the wood paneling are stone," Beau said. "You won't find anything hollow there."

"If I do," Kaye said, "it might be a secret panel with treasure hidden behind it."

"You think the king hid the treasure in the walls?" I said, going over to him.

"All the castle walls are very thick," he said, his face bright and interested-looking. It reminded me of when I first met him and he wasn't worried all the time about his father and war and losing his knighthood. "It would be the perfect place to hide a treasure. That's where I would have hidden it if I were the old king."

I stared at Kaye. Something he said sounded really important, but I didn't know why. "If you were the old king," I said slowly. "But you're not the old king."

Kaye laughed. "I know. I just thought that he would also know that the walls are a great place to hide treasure. Let's split up and start searching. Check all the wood panels, and come get me if you find anything unusual."

He mapped out the different parts of the castle and assigned each of us areas to search every day after lessons. Kaye even talked Abelard into sending us food each afternoon. Usually Tom Spot brought it to us.

Working by myself was boring. Every afternoon I thumped and pounded wooden panels until my fist felt like a giant bruise. It was also lonely, so I was glad whenever Tom showed up.

One afternoon, about two days before the messengers from Eldridge were supposed to arrive, Tom brought me my afternoon snack. "How's the search, Master Reggie?" he asked. "Find anything unusual?" Tom was very familiar with Kaye's instructions. Every afternoon, Kaye asked Tom to remind us to come get him if we found anything suspicious.

"No," I said. "Nothing ever happens."

Tom held out the food packet. "There's blackberries today. Me and Embert and Tom picked them this morning."

Even that didn't cheer me up. "I wish I could pick berries," I said. "I hate knocking on these stupid walls every day."

"I can help you thump," Tom said. "Master Abelard won't miss me for a while yet."

That did cheer me up a little bit. "Great!" I said, giving three good bangs to the wall in front of me. "But I just finished in here."

"Where to next?" Tom asked.

"I have to check the passage outside this room next. There's lots of paneling to thump out there."

We stepped into the hallway and Tom looked around. "This is the clean hallway," he said slowly.

It took me a moment to realize what he meant. It was the hallway where I had made the dust angels and seen the spook's footprints.

"Well, we already know there's something unusual about this place," I said, starting to thump on the paneling. My fist made the noise I was so tired of hearing: clump, clump, clump.

"Aye," Tom said. "Did you ever tell Sir Kaye about it?" He began thumping the panels on the other side of the hall. Clump, clump, clump.

"No. He doesn't like to hear about the spooks. He thinks I'm crazy."

"Crazy?" Tom said. "Even after the spook made the drawing in the dust?"

I shrugged. "He thinks it was Melchor trying to trick him."

Tom nodded. "Aye, Sir Melchor's bragging all around the castle how he's going to get Sir Kaye sent home crying. But Sir Kaye should listen to you."

"That would be nice," I said as I kept hitting the wall. Clump, clump, clump, *clomp.* I froze.

I tried again. Clump, clump, *clomp*.

"Tom! Listen! Does that sound hollow to you?"

"Aye, it does for sure, Master Reggie!" Tom cried. "How big is the hollow place?"

I thumped some more and found that the hollow area was at the bottom of the wall. It was about as wide as my arm was long and as high as my waist when I stood up.

"What do you think it is?" I asked.

"Maybe it's the treasure," Tom said excitedly. "Should we go find Sir Kaye?"

"Not yet. Let's see if we can open this. If we find the treasure inside, we'll close it up again and get Kaye."

Tom grinned and felt around the edges of the hollow area. "Maybe there's a door that swings out if we pull on it," he said.

I squinted at the wood paneling. It was old and cracked in places, but mostly smooth all over. "There's nothing to pull on, Tom."

"Then maybe we push?" he said, throwing his whole body against the wall. When that didn't work, he banged on it as hard as he could. Nothing happened except a lot of noise.

Finally Tom gave up and leaned against the wall. "I don't know what else to try, Master Reggie. Maybe we should get Sir Kaye and let him—"

Tom never finished his sentence. His face went gray and his eyes bulged like a beetle's eyes. He pointed to his ear pressed tightly against the wall. "I thought I heard something," he said. "Something like a scratching noise."

I shuddered. "Something like rats?" I asked. "Because if it's rats, I say we let Kaye open it first."

"Just listen, Master Reggie, please." He sounded a lot like me whenever I tried telling Kaye about the spook.

I put my ear against the paneling and listened hard. "I don't hear any scratching," I said. But then I heard something worse— a voice, whispering straight into my ear in a way that made my skin shiver. "Reggieeee,"it breathed. Then, "Tommmm."

"Aaaaahhhh!" We jumped to our feet and tore down the long passage, running faster than rabbits trying to escape from Oriana.

# chapter twenty-one

"Wait!" I cried, skidding to a stop. I had an idea. Tom turned around, his white face dripping with sweat. I felt bad for him, so I said, "Tom, you go on. I have to go back. If that's the spook, it might know where the treasure is. If we can find out, Kaye can stay a knight—it's the most important thing in the world to him. I have to try."

Tom nodded, but didn't say anything.

I turned around and walked back, clenching my jaw to stop my teeth from dancing against each other. Tom followed a long way behind me, which helped me feel a little more brave, although my knees still quivered like custard.

When I reached the hollow panel, I made my hands into fists and hollered, "I'm not afraid of you! I need your help!"

I knelt by the panel and said, "Are you still there? Can you help me?"

Nothing happened.

"Please, Friend. I need you." I heard the faint scratching noise again, but nothing else. I tried one last time. "Are you there, Friend?"

"Yessss," the scary whispering voice said. It sounded faint—almost like the wind, except this wind had words in it.

I shivered, wrapped my arms around my chest, and pressed my ear to the wall. "I have some questions. First, is the lost treasure behind this panel?"

"Noooo," the voice said.

I tried again. "Do you know where the treasure is hidden?"

"Noooo."

"Do you know what the clue 'silent arrow' means?"

After a short pause, the soft voice said, "Noooo."

"Ratfingers," I heard Tom mutter. I thought I heard a breathy chuckle behind the wall, but I couldn't be sure.

"Is there anything behind this panel that will help Kaye find the treasure?" I asked.

"Noooo," the voice breathed.

I hit my knees with my fists. "I don't know what else to ask!" I cried. I heard the little scratching noise again, so I called out, "Wait! Don't go! Thank you. Are—are we friends?"

I waited, my ears filling up with silence. I was about to give up when the soft answer came, saying, "Yessss." I heard the scratching noise again and then nothing.

I had been holding my breath the whole time. I let it out in a big sigh and heard Tom do the same. I saw that he also had his ear pushed up against the wall.

"Um, would you say that was unusual?" I asked him.

"Let's get Sir Kaye," he said.

In a few moments, the four of us gathered around the panel. Kaye didn't believe we had talked with the spook. He was, however, very excited about the hollow place behind the wood paneling. He knocked and thumped and listened. "This could be it, Reggie!" he said.

The wood paneling only covered the bottom half of the wall. Kaye glanced at the top of it and inspected the bottom. He found a tiny gap next to the floor, fit his fingers into it, and slid the whole panel straight up the wall, revealing a dark space behind.

Tom whistled. "I never thought of that," he said.

We crawled into a narrow, empty space. There was no sign of the spook, so I didn't say anything. I didn't want to aggravate Kaye. At the far end of the room, a single arrow slit let in a little light. Grit covered the floor and made a scratching noise as we walked.

We could see the castle courtyard through the arrow loop. Melchor stood next to a wagon, supervising the unloading of some heavy boxes.

"What's he doing?" I asked.

Beau said, "Those boxes are full of Melchor's money. He brought it here to pay Eldridge."

"Too bad there isn't any treasure here," Kaye said sadly. "I really thought there would be."

"What's this place for?" Tom asked. "It's just an empty room."

"Maybe it's for spying on the courtyard," Beau said as we left the room and slid the panel shut.

"Beg pardon, Your Grace," Tom said, "I have to go back. Master Abelard will be right angry if I stay gone. He needs help cooking the feast for the Eldridge messengers. They're coming day after tomorrow. There's lots to do."

"Bye, Tom," Beau said. I waved.

Kaye's face looked like someone had taken a wet rag and washed all the color off of it. I thought he was going to be sick. I started to worry that it just might kill him if he didn't find that treasure soon.

"Come on, Kaye, don't give up," Beau said, giving him several hearty slaps on the back. "Let's go to the gallery and search some more."

Kaye looked dizzy after the slaps, but the color came back into his face. "That's right," he said. "We never finished searching in there."

The gallery wasn't the only place we hadn't finished searching. Talking to the spook and finding a secret spy chamber was so exciting that I forgot to finish searching the hallway. I had forgotten that the footprints I found when making dust angels led straight across the hallway. I never thought that if there was a sliding panel on one side of the corridor, there was probably an identical one on the other side.

It would have been better if I had remembered.

# chapter twenty-two

That night I had a terrible nightmare. In my dream, Kaye and Beau and I were in the gallery. Kaye was talking about the walls, saying, "If I were the old king, that's where I'd hide my treasure." Then he started laughing like a crazy person until he laughed himself to pieces. All the pieces of Kaye turned into wooden falcon carvings, but the carvings were alive. They came at me, and I was afraid they were going to peck my eyes out.

I yelled and sat up in bed, breathing hard. I was upset by my dream, but I had learned something. All this time we had been thinking like Kaye—how Kaye would have hidden the treasure if he had been the old king. We needed to think like the old king himself. Where would *he* have hidden the treasure?

I realized Kaye wasn't in the room. I took a candle and went looking for him. I walked up and down clammy stone halls until my feet almost froze, which made me wish for a pair of boot-stockings like the queen's. I couldn't find Kaye anywhere. I finally had to give up and go back to bed to get warm again.

I woke up the next morning when Kaye stumbled into the room. Dark shadows filled the spaces under his eyes, and he looked pale and sick. Dust and cobwebs coated his clothes like a fragile suit of armor.

"Where have you been?" I asked.

"Searching," he said, lowering himself onto the bed.

"Did you find anything?"

Kaye closed his eyes and said, "No." He sounded old and tired.

"How much of the castle is left to search?" I asked.

Half asleep, Kaye muttered, "Most of it."

"That's going to take forever," I said. Kaye only snored in reply.

I went to meet Beau and Alchir in the library, leaving Kaye fast asleep with his mouth hanging open.

We had lessons without Kaye. He joined us shortly before midday, yawning and looking worse than half-chewed hay.

Alchir didn't say anything about Kaye's lateness. Instead, he gave Kaye an assignment and sat down to read a book. Kaye picked up a pen and put it down again. He shook his head a few times and blinked really hard. Then he rested his head face-down on the table.

Now that everyone was finally here, I told them about my dream and my idea to start thinking less like Kaye and more like the old king.

"I don't see how we can figure out how the old king thought if none of us ever met him," Kaye said without lifting his head.

"You have to use your imagination," I said.

Kaye snorted. "Imagination! We need facts. We'll never find a treasure by just imagining it."

"Fine," I said. "Then let's think of the facts we know about the old king."

"He's dead," Beau said.

I frowned. "What else do we know?"

"He was sick for a long time before he died," Kaye mumbled into the table.

"Good," I said. "What else?"

Beau waved his hand at me. "He liked falcons."

I thought for a minute. "He loved his library."

"And books," Beau said. "Those are probably the two things he loved best—falcons and books."

"That's right!" I said to Beau. "He even wrote a book about all his falcons. I saved it for you, since you like falcons too." I laughed. "You should see the way he tried to draw his falcons in the book. They were so bad. That's how I knew the first clue was a falcon." I slapped the table. "That's another thing we know about the king! He's terrible at drawing."

Kaye lifted his head off the table. "Wait a minute. Can I see the book? If it helped you figure out the first clue, maybe there's something else in it that will help us."

"Of course," I said, and ran to get the book from its hiding place. Kaye and Beau started leafing through it together.

"He does know a lot about training falcons," Beau said. "I think I'll try some of his ideas when I get my new falcon."

Kaye kept turning pages. "Now he's writing about all his different falcons. Especially his gyrfalcons. He really liked them."

Beau poked his finger at one of the pages. "Look at that." He looked up at me. "Remember that perch in the mews with the name Delilah carved over it?" He turned a few pages. "The king wrote pages and pages here about how amazing Delilah was. It's almost like a love letter."

"I know someone else who's written a letter to a bird," I said.

Beau laughed and said, "Yes. Well. The king must have been a very clever and charming man, much like myself. And Delilah must have been his favorite bird."

"You're not joking," Kaye said. "You should see all the nicknames he has for Delilah. He calls her his noble fowl." Kaye kept flipping through the book and reading off nicknames. "His bountiful huntress...his precious pet..."

We started snickering.

"His sweetest love…"

I had to lean on the table, I was laughing so hard, but I finally calmed down enough to ask, "What else, Kaye?"

Kaye shouted, "Fancy feathers!" I could hardly hear him because we were laughing so hard, but he yelled out, "Here's another one!" But instead of reading it to us, he stopped laughing and stared at the book so hard that his chin stuck out like a gargoyle.

"So what is it?" Beau asked.

Kaye swallowed hard and finally looked up at us. "He—he calls her his silent arrow."

"What?" we cried out. "Show us."

Kaye pointed at the spindly writing. I couldn't read it, but Beau read out loud, "Oh, Delilah, my silent arrow, how swift and fierce you fly to the heart of your prey."

"Ugh," I said, wrinkling my nose. "Was he trying to write a song about her? It's terrible. Poor King Frederic. He was kind of bad at everything."

Beau and Kaye stared at me. "Reggie," Beau said, "the silent arrow—it's Delilah."

It took me a moment to understand what he meant. My mouth dropped open. "The second clue!" I yelled. "Let's go!"

# chapter twenty-three

We dropped the book on the table and ran to the mews. Kaye and Beau crossed the courtyard so fast their feet never seemed to touch the ground.

I ran behind them, concentrating so hard on keeping up with them that I didn't see Milo step out of the barracks. I banged into him. He grabbed the back of my shirt to stop me from running any farther.

"So, Dogtail, I see you're trailing behind the others as usual," he said. Then he chuckled. "Or maybe I should say 'tailing' behind the others, you useless brat."

"Let go of me!" I said, twisting away from him.

"What are you three after?" he asked, but I didn't answer. When I reached the mews, Kaye and Beau were banging all over the wood paneling around Delilah's perch.

"It's hollow from top to bottom here, Reggie, listen," Beau said, pounding the wall for me. Oriana lifted her wings and bristled. She did not appreciate the noise.

Beau tried to calm her while Kaye studied the wall.

"Will it open?" I asked.

"We'll see," he said. He tried sliding it up the wall. When that didn't work, he tried pulling and pushing on Delilah's perch. Nothing happened. Kaye tried everything he could think of to open that wall. Finally, when Beau pulled on the perch while Kaye pushed hard against the wall near the floor, the wall moved.

The top half swung down, while the bottom half swung in. I saw steps going down into darkness and nothing else.

"We did it," Kaye said with a grin. All his sleepiness had disappeared. He started walking down the stairs, but Beau pulled him back.

"We'll need lights," he said. "Good ones."

"I know where to get some," I said. "There's a box in the old king's room full of those good fat king candles. I'll be right back."

I ran all the way up to the king's room, got the box of candles and some holders, and ran back down. I wanted to stop in the kitchen and get some provisions—maybe some bread and cold meat and fruit. Good explorers always carry provisions, but I didn't want to make Kaye wait any longer to find that treasure.

I passed Sir Milo in the courtyard again. He sat on a box, leaning against a wall, with his arms crossed over his chest. His eyes narrowed when he saw the box I carried. I was glad he didn't say anything to me this time.

While I was gone, Beau had found a torch, which he used to light two of the candles. Giving one to me, he kept one for himself and handed the torch to Kaye, who started down the stairs.

"Don't close the door all the way," Kaye told Beau, who came last. "We might not be able to open it from the inside. We wouldn't want to get trapped down here."

Beau propped the door open with one of the candles. We took the rest with us.

The narrow steps went down and down and down between two stone walls. The damp air smelled musty. My head started to hurt, but soon a tiny breeze blew past our faces, freshening the air and making the flames of the candles flutter like bright moth wings.

The stairs finally ended. We took a few steps forward and the path got wider and higher. The walls were now rock, not man-built stone. We were in some kind of cave tunnel! I heard water dripping in the distance.

"This," Kaye said, grinning, "is the perfect place to hide a treasure. Let's go!"

We followed the tunnel for a long way. Small rock rooms and large caverns opened off it from time to time, but the main tunnel was mostly straight and flat. Someone, once upon a time, had worked really hard to make the floor smooth and level. I didn't realize how smooth it was until I stumbled over the loose stones of a rockslide. I lost my footing and dropped my candle, which went out. Kaye silently pulled me up while Beau relit my candle, and we pushed through the soot-black darkness like nothing had happened.

Finally, we saw daylight through a narrow opening and Kaye said, "This tunnel must be a secret escape route in case the castle is ever conquered."

We squeezed through the gap in the tunnel wall and popped out into some bushes at the edge of a forest. The bushes overlooked a shallow green valley dotted with white sheep in the sunlight. A nearby stream flowed out of the forest and through the meadow.

"I guess we don't have to worry about getting trapped in the tunnel," I said, looking up. White clouds floated in the high perfect blue like little sky sheep. It was a beautiful day to be outside, but all three of us turned around and headed back into the cave.

By the time my eyes adjusted to the dark, I realized Kaye had opened a small wooden door set into the tunnel wall. I hadn't noticed it before.

"Is it the treasure?" I asked.

"No," Kaye said, lifting his torch so he could see better. "It's—it's a house." He sounded surprised.

"What!" I ran inside to look. Behind the door, a short tunnel led to a cozy looking cave where I saw a hearth and chimney and a bed. Shelves carved into the rock held ripening cheeses, a

cooking pot or two, and wooden boxes. Bunches of dried herbs hung from the ceiling. A chest stood against one of the cave walls with firewood stacked on one side of it. Small oak casks on the other side of the chest smelled of ale brewing. A table and a few stools filled the rest of the space.

Beau sniffed at the ale casks, "Whew. That's strong stuff."

I sniffed too. The air smelled delicious—fresh and clean, with warm, smoky scents of spices and ale and cheeses and herbs and honey mixed in.

"The hearth is still warm," Kaye said. "I wonder who lives here."

I lifted the cover off a wooden box on the table and almost dropped it when a familiar flowery smell rose to meet my nose. A whole box of spook sweets! Was this where the spook lived? I kept my mouth shut. I didn't feel like being laughed at.

We decided to search the rest of the tunnel. Most of the openings along it led to small, man-made storerooms carved out of the rock. We searched all of them, but we didn't find any treasure. "We should search the real caves," Beau said. "There are probably lots of hiding places in there."

Two natural caverns branched off the tunnel. Compared to the storerooms, the caverns felt immense, stretching into darkness and making our candles about as useful as a handful of fireflies. We worked our way around the edges of the first cavern, peering into every nook and cranny we could find.

Hour after hour after hour we crept slowly around the cavern. I wished more than ever that I had brought some food. Kaye's torch burned out and we were down to our last candle when we finally reached the tunnel again.

Beau sighed. "Well at least we made it back before we ran out of candles."

"We still need to search the middle of the cave," Kaye said, lifting the last candle and walking into the center of the darkness. I went with him, but Beau grabbed Kaye's arm and pulled him back into the tunnel.

"Not without better light," he said. "Come on, Reggie."

I took one step farther into the cave, so I could brag to the Toms and Embert, but I tripped and fell, jostling some pebbles loose. They rolled across the floor and after a brief pause, I heard the noise of rock hitting rock.

"Hey! Bring that candle here!" I yelled. As soon as I had some light, I saw that the cavern floor sloped downhill to a good-sized hole in the cave floor. If I had fallen into it, I would never have gotten out by myself.

Beau whistled. "Good thing you didn't fall in. We're leaving now. No one's coming back until we have more lights." He marched us back to the door to the mews. At the top of the stairs, Beau stopped. "That's funny. The door's shut. I know I propped it open with a candle."

# CHAPTER twenty-four

Beau moved the candle around the edges of the door. "Aha!" he said. "There's a handle here." He grabbed a loop of rope attached to the bottom of the door and gave it a sharp tug. The panel popped open and we crawled out to see Oriana flying madly around the top of the room, bouncing off walls and perches.

"There, there, my girl," Beau said to her softly, closing the wall with a gentle push. "I know you don't like having the walls of your house burst open. But aren't you glad I'm back?"

Oriana slowed down and eventually sat on one perch, glaring at us, first with one eye, then the other, turning her head sharply from side to side. Beau continued soothing her while Kaye looked around. Finally, in the farthest corner of the room, he bent and picked up a candle—our missing door prop.

"This didn't roll over here by accident," he said. "Look."

Part of a dirty boot print marked the smooth wax of the candle.

"Someone kicked it?" Beau asked.

Kaye nodded.

"Milo could have done it," I said. "He was in the courtyard this afternoon. Maybe he wondered why we went into the mews and never came out."

Kaye slapped his forehead. "We should have been more careful. I was so excited about the clue that I forgot that someone might follow us."

"Don't worry," Beau said. "If we didn't find anything down there today, Milo won't either. Let's go get some food."

"Food! I'm starving!" I said, racing to the door. I was the first one out, but two steps later I stopped. Kaye and Beau crashed into me. "He's still there," I whispered.

Milo sat on his box, leaning against the wall, arms folded across his chest, looking exactly the same as he did when I last saw him. "He's been sitting there for hours," I said.

Milo stood up and strolled toward us. "You've been in there a long time," he said. "What's so interesting about the mews?"

"Falcons," Beau said innocently.

"For hours?" Milo said, raising one eyebrow.

"Oh, yes," Beau said. "Falcons are fascinating. We even found a book in the library this morning written by the old king himself. He went on for pages and pages, all about his special falcons."

Milo folded his long arms again. "You found that book this morning, just before you ran down here and spent the entire day in the falcon mews?"

"That's right," I said, talking very fast. "We just can't get enough falconry." Even I didn't believe me.

Milo flicked a glance at me. "Quiet, Dogtail. I'm not interested in you." He grunted and eyeballed Kaye. "Shouldn't you be looking for that treasure? Or did you finally have the sense to give up?"

Kaye took a step forward and folded his own arms. "I don't give up," he said. "I'll find that treasure. Nothing's going to stop me."

Grinning, Milo relaxed and said, "So you didn't find it yet."

"No, but trust me, I will."

Milo laughed, looking like a donkey braying. "Trust you?" he said. "Not even the queen trusts you. She's sorry she ever knighted you. Why do you think she was so quick to go along with Melchor's idea to send you home? She can't wait to get rid of you! You're no knight. You're a disappointment." Milo strode off into the darkness.

Kaye opened his mouth and shut it a few times, like a fish tasting the air and finding it unpleasant. Then his shoulders slumped. "Let's just go eat," he said.

"Don't listen to him, Kaye," Beau said. "The queen didn't make you a knight because she wanted you to find the treasure. She never asked you to find it. You offered."

"I'm not doing a very good job," he said, "and the messengers from Eldridge will be here tomorrow. It's too late. I've failed."

"No you haven't," I said. "It's not too late until the queen gives them Melchor's money. You have all night and most of the day tomorrow. You could still find it."

"Maybe," Kaye said, but he looked more hopeful as we entered the great hall to cross to the kitchen on the other side.

# chapter twenty-five

The queen was leaving the great hall when we entered. We had been so busy hunting for treasure that I hadn't seen her in a while. Now I stared at her in surprise.

She looked thin—too thin. Her eyes seemed bigger and they shone with a glassy light. A deep crease had formed between her eyebrows, and as she passed us, she held a hand to her side like she was in pain. I saw tiny speckles of color scattered across her fingers. She must have been painting at night again. No wonder she looked so tired.

Kaye brightened when he saw her, "Your Majesty," he said, running up to her, "you won't believe what we found!"

The queen looked at Kaye like she couldn't understand him. She blinked twice like it was hard work and finally seemed to recognize him.

"Oh, Kaye. Not now," she said with a sigh. "Later." She wandered upstairs like she was walking through a dream. Kaye stared after her with a hurt look on his face.

Beau said, "Something's wrong. I'm going after her." He started for the stairs, but Kaye dashed past him.

All thoughts of food forgotten, I climbed the stairs too. I reached the top just in time to see Kaye run up the next staircase, probably heading for the library, while Beau hurried toward the queen's apartments. Curious about the queen, I decided to follow Beau.

"Is my aunt all right?" he asked Nicolette through the doorway of the queen's bedchamber.

"She's not well," Nicolette said. "She made herself sick by staying up late painting again, and ever since she heard that Dworfurd escaped, she's gotten worse. Let her rest tonight. You can talk to her tomorrow."

Nicolette waved us away and shut the door, so we found a candle and went after Kaye. By the time we reached the dark library, he was feeling all over our lesson table with his hands like a blind man.

"Bring the light closer," he said. He picked up two books lying on the table and glared at them before slapping them down again. "Where is it?" he asked in a tense whisper.

"Where is what?" Beau asked.

"The king's falcon book. Maybe there's something in it that will help me find the treasure in the caves."

"We left it on the table today," I said. "It should still be there."

"Look in your hiding place," he said. "Maybe you put it back."

I emptied my secret spot, bringing out the book about Sir Gregory and the boring but beautiful jeweled book. "It's not here," I said, putting my other two books on the table. Beau set the candle down, making shadows flicker upwards onto Kaye's face.

"Oh, no," Kaye said. "I need it." He picked up the Sir Gregory book and flipped through a few pages. The candle flame wavered and the shadow of his nose bobbed up and down on his forehead. I was so busy watching his nose shadow that I didn't realize Kaye was talking to me.

"Why didn't you show me that book days ago? We could have found the treasure by now. You had enough sense to realize the king's bad drawings were falcons. Why couldn't you have had enough sense to show me *how* you knew that?"

"I didn't know it was such an important book," I said.

Kaye slammed the Sir Gregory book onto the table. "You thought it was important enough to hide," he said. "Did Melchor or Milo tell you to hide it? Were you spying for them?"

"Are you crazy?" I cried. "I would never do that! I saved the book for Beau because he likes falcons. I didn't know it was important. I couldn't read it. It was too hard."

"Well maybe you should learn to read," Kaye said in a cold voice that didn't sound like his.

Beau said, "Kaye! Don't be angry at Reggie. We would have never even seen the book without him. He saved the day by showing it to us this morning."

"He could have showed me the book weeks ago," Kaye said, almost yelling. "And you're no better, Beau. Milo's not stupid. He knows we found a secret staircase in the mews. You practically told him the king's falcon book helped us find it. He probably came up here and stole it so we couldn't use it anymore."

Beau blushed. "I didn't think of that."

"Well you should have," Kaye said. "That book was my last chance to get help finding the treasure."

"We'll help you, Kaye," I said. "We can search all night if we have to."

"No," he said, walking to the door, looking red and angry. "They're right, you know. All you do is follow me around and get in the way. I don't need your help, Dogtail. I'll find that treasure by myself."

# chapter twenty-six

I stared after him, my mouth hanging open. I wanted to cry, but I couldn't, because I seemed to be frozen. Finally I melted enough to move my head. I looked at Beau.

He looked frozen too, but he could talk. "He didn't mean it, Reggie. He's upset."

Now I was melting too much, especially around my knees, so I sat down. "I try to help," I said. "I try to tell him things all the time, but he never listens. I don't know what to do. Maybe—maybe I should go home."

Beau sat down in another chair and leaned his head on his hand. "I wish you'd both stay," he said, "but I know Kaye won't want to live here if he's not a knight anymore." He sighed, and the candle flame flapped and fluttered like a banner in a breeze. "Sometimes I feel like I only make friends to lose them," he said.

I found my green bead in my pocket and pulled it out. I folded my hand around it and held it for a moment before asking, "Who did you lose?"

"I left friends behind when I came to Knox," he said, "but my mother died when I was born. My uncle died a few years ago. He was more like a father to me than my own father, but now he's gone. I miss him."

I chewed on my bottom lip, thinking. "You haven't lost us," I finally said. "I'm still your friend. And maybe we can both still be Kaye's friends, if he'll let us."

Beau nodded. "Maybe. I'm not hungry anymore," he said. "I'm going to bed."

"Go ahead," I said. "I'll stay here."

"I'm taking the candle," he said, standing up. "Won't you be afraid in the dark? What about your spook?"

I shrugged. "There are worse things than spooks," I said. "Things like best friends who never listen and then get mad and call you names."

After hesitating a moment, Beau said, "Well, if you're sure you'll be all right."

I put my books away. "I'll be fine," I said. He left, taking the candle with him. Everything went black, but soon I could see cold blue moonlight pouring through the windows. It was so quiet and sad that I just couldn't stay there any longer.

I walked through familiar halls to the tower room. It was empty. I couldn't believe how mean Kaye had been. I had never heard him say anything like that to anyone. I fell asleep wondering if everyone who knew me figured out sooner or later that I was mostly useless.

The next morning I opened my eyes and saw the sunlight sifting through the open window, lighting up all the floating bits of dust in the air.

It felt like a long time had passed since I had seen the sun yesterday over the sheep meadow. I blinked in the strong light. I had slept longer than I meant to.

While pulling on my boots I remembered what day it was—today was the day the messengers from Eldridge were coming for their money. And today was the last day Kaye would ever be a knight. I wondered if he was still searching in the caves and if he was still angry at me and Beau.

I found Beau in the great hall, helping the Toms set up long tables for the feast. The room was full of workers, including some of the knights. I saw Sir Griswald helping Embert spread white cloths over the tables. Alfred carried a big basket of fresh herbs that he scattered into the rushes on the floor. The herbs would make the hall smell nice for the feast. Even Milo carried benches into the hall, tucking them under his long arms.

I saw Melchor leaning against a doorway, surveying the whole scene with a pleased look on his face.

I finally had a chance to get Beau's attention. "What's *he* doing here?" I said, pointing at Melchor.

He chuckled sadly. "I think he wants to make sure everything is perfect for his big day."

"His big day?"

"Today he gets to be the hero and save the kingdom from war by giving the queen his money for Eldridge," he said.

"He gets to get rid of Kaye today too," I said.

Beau shook his head. "Poor Kaye. He must feel awful."

"Where is he?" I asked.

"I don't know," Beau said.

Milo walked by and sneered. "I know where he is."

"Where?" I asked.

Milo grinned. "Kaye's gone," he said so loudly that everyone in the hall heard him. "He ran away. He couldn't stand to fail, so he disappeared."

I stared at him. "Kaye wouldn't run away. He's not a coward!"

With a smirk, Milo said, "If only cowards run away, then your friend's a coward, because he ran. I saw him."

"Maybe he couldn't bear to say goodbye to us," Melchor called out, "because he would miss us too much."

They both laughed so loudly I could feel the hot air from Milo's mouth move my hair.

Milo added, "It serves him right for thinking he could beat a great knight like Melchor at anything real. Little Kaye just doesn't have what it takes to be a knight. Good thing he won't have to worry about that after today."

Now some of the knights in the room were laughing, but I noticed Sir Griswald wasn't. Tom Spot scowled at the floor as he worked. Alfred didn't even crack a smile. Of course, Alfred never smiled.

I grabbed Beau's elbow and pulled him out to the courtyard. "Something's wrong, Beau. Kaye wouldn't run away. It's not like him."

"Reggie, he was really upset last night. He wasn't acting like himself. He might have gone home," Beau said.

"He wouldn't do that!" I said. "I *tried* to talk him into going home—more than once—but he wouldn't even think about it. Kaye doesn't give up. If Milo hadn't said anything to us, where would you think Kaye was right now?"

"In the caves, looking for treasure," Beau said.

"See! I know he's there. Milo only said he ran away so we'd look for Kaye in the wrong place. He's in trouble, Beau. We have to find him."

"I'll get some torches and meet you in the mews as soon as I can," Beau said, running off toward the armory.

Trying to look unimportant, I hurried through the great hall and into the kitchen. Roasting meats sizzled and pots bubbled and everything smelled wonderful, but I only stayed long enough to grab some provisions and tuck them into a bag. Tom Spot saw what I was doing and slipped me a few raisin tarts.

"Go find Sir Kaye, Master Reggie. There's no way he ran away," he said.

By the time I left the kitchen, the messengers from Eldridge had been sighted, traveling slowly up the road to the castle. A guard on the gatehouse tower blew a trumpet blast in greeting. No one noticed me as I slipped through the gathering crowds and disappeared into the falcon mews.

# chapter twenty-seven

Back in the tunnel, the torches burned so much brighter than candles. When Beau and I stepped into the big cave with the hole, we were amazed to see the cavern's arches soaring high above our heads.

"Should we look in this big cave or the other one?" I asked.

"If Kaye was down here all night," Beau said, "he probably finished searching this cave. Let's look in the other one."

We turned to go, but stopped when we heard the sound of rocks rolling on rocks. "Kaye," I called, "are you in here?"

Now we heard a sound like someone kicking a stone across a courtyard.

"It's coming from the hole," Beau said. I ran to the edge and leaned over with a torch. Kaye lay on his back in the bottom of the pit. Strong ropes tied his hands and feet together as he tried kicking at the rocks in the pit. A cloth wrapped around his mouth muffled his yells.

"Kaye!" I cried out. "I knew something was wrong! What happened to you?"

He glared at me. I guess it was kind of silly to try to ask him questions when his mouth was tied up.

"We need rope," Beau said. "I know where to find some. I'll be right back."

I examined the pit. The straight sides were smooth and hard to climb, but it was more than just a pit. It extended back into the cave like a small canyon. I walked deeper into the cave, following the edge of the hole. At the back, the straight edges of the pit gave way to a slope of loose rocks that led all the way to the bottom of the pit.

I carefully tossed my torch into the pit and climbed down the slope. Little rocks rolled and bounced off each other, skittering

downward. I slid down with them to the bottom of the hole. Fortunately I landed on top of the rocks and not underneath them.

Standing up, I felt my arms and legs. Nothing was damaged, so I tried climbing back up the slope. It was impossible. The rocks rolled under my feet and I kept sliding back into the pit. I would have to wait until Beau brought the rope.

I grabbed my torch and ran to where Kaye lay bound and gagged. Pulling a little knife from my belt, I soon cut him free.

He sat up, but he looked funny.

"Are you hurt?" I asked.

"No. Everything's spinning," he said, scooting backwards to lean against the wall of the pit.

"You need to eat," I told him, handing him a chunk of hard cheese and some dried apple slices from my bag. He chewed on them in silence for a while, and the color came back to his face. By the time he finished a raisin tart, he looked almost normal again. I ate a tart or two to keep him company.

"What happened?" I asked. "Did Milo do this to you?"

"Milo and two others," he said in a faint voice. "I think they were castle guards. Last night they followed me down here and tied me up and lowered me into this pit. Milo was worried I'd find the treasure at the last minute. He wanted to keep me out of the way until it was too late for me to ruin Melchor's big day. Then he went back upstairs and left the guards to make sure I didn't escape."

"Where are they now?" I asked.

"They got bored and went exploring," Kaye said.

"I hope Beau brings the rope before they come back," I said.

Kaye shrugged. "They won't hurt us. Milo knows the queen said she'd take away the lands of any knight who hurts me. He was very careful not to bump or bruise me when they put me down here. But it doesn't matter now. I don't care what they do to me."

"What do you mean?"

"The Eldridge people are here now, aren't they?" Kaye asked.

"Probably," I said. "They were almost here when we came down to look for you."

Kaye pulled his knees to his chest and wrapped his arms around his legs. "So that's it then," he said. "I'm not a knight anymore."

He bit his lips and stared into the dark with a blank expression on his face. He sat like that for so long that I started to worry. In the sputtering torchlight he looked like a wood carving of a scrawny old goblin.

The silence in the cave pressed down on me until I felt nervous. All I could hear was my own breathing, and it sounded too loud and too fast. It didn't help that Kaye kept sitting there like a dead person.

I poked him in the arm. Nothing happened. I took hold of his shoulders and shook him a little. "Kaye, Kaye, it's me, Reggie. Are you all right?"

Kaye blinked a few times and looked at me. Finally he took a deep breath and said, "Why are you here?"

"You disappeared, so we came looking for you," I answered slowly, worried he had hit his head when he landed down here.

"But I was mean to you. I called you Dogtail. I know that makes you feel bad. I'm sorry. I don't think I was a very good knight. And I know I wasn't a good friend."

Surprised, I asked, "How do you know it makes me feel bad? I thought I hid it from everyone."

In a tired voice, Kaye said, "When someone makes you feel really bad, you always take something out of your pocket and start rolling it between your fingers. What is it?"

"It's a glass bead," I said, but I didn't explain it. Instead I said, "I can't believe you know that. I didn't even know I did that."

"You're my best friend, Reggie," Kaye said. "Of course I see the things you do."

"But you don't always hear the words I say," I said, and found myself reaching into my pocket for the bead. I stopped, suddenly angry that Kaye knew all kinds of things about me, but never seemed to listen to me.

"What do you mean?" he asked.

I told him everything I had discovered about the spook. For the first time, he didn't interrupt me to tell me there were no such things as spooks. At the end, he said, "You were right. I should have listened to you. Someone is definitely sneaking around the castle."

"So you don't think I'm crazy?" I asked.

"I never did. But you do like to imagine things. Sometimes you get a little carried away with that."

"Maybe," I said, "but after seeing the cave house, I don't think it's a spook anymore. It's a real person. You were right about that."

Kaye didn't say anything. "Kaye?" I said, worried that he was acting like a wood carving again.

"Sshhh," he whispered. "Do you hear something?"

I heard some noises echoing through the cave. After a moment, I realized it was someone singing loudly. He sounded worse than Beau's lute when it needed to be tuned.

"It's the guards!" Kaye whispered. "Quick, tie me up again and put out the torch and hide!"

I covered Kaye's mouth with the cloth and wrapped the rope loosely around his hands and feet so he looked like he was still tied up. Then I hid at the back of the pit and put out the torch.

A man appeared, carrying a torch. He leaned over the edge of the pit and leered at Kaye. "He's still here!" he yelled over his shoulder. No one answered. The man gave a huge belch that echoed through the cave. "Now don't you go anywhere," he said, shaking his finger at Kaye. "We've found a better place to wait, but we'll come back for you later."

With a gentle hiccup, he wandered back into the tunnel. The light from his torch dipped up and down and waved back and forth as he made his unsteady way back to wherever he came from.

When he left, the dark swallowed me up. "Kaye?" I called.

"Here, Reggie, follow my voice," Kaye said. He kept talking until I made it to the front of the pit, where a faint scent of ale lingered in the cool air.

I sniffed. "Smells like they found the spook's ale," I said.

Kaye coughed. "You should be glad you were at the back of the pit when he belched. If I didn't have that cloth over my face, I think I would have been sick."

I laughed. We were trapped in a pit, in possibly the darkest cave in the world, but it was nice to have my friend back.

# chapter twenty-eight

A few minutes later, the dark seemed to lessen a little, and shortly after that, I saw another torch. I didn't have time to hide.

"I hope it's Beau this time," I said.

It was. In no time he lowered a rope and helped us climb out.

"I didn't have any trouble getting the rope," Beau said as I lit my torch from his. "The courtyard is empty, except for Oliphus, who's lurking about. Everyone else is at the feast. The minstrels sound amazing. I wish I could get my lute and play with them. The visitors from Eldridge are having a fine time. I didn't realize there would be so many of them."

"They need lots of people to protect the money from bandits on the way back to Eldridge," I said.

Kaye sighed. "Too bad it's Melchor's money."

"I'm sorry, Kaye," I said. "We tried really hard to find the treasure. We just needed more time."

He shrugged his shoulders. "Well, we have lots of time now that I'm not a knight anymore. Maybe we should keep looking. Queen Vianne still needs money to run her kingdom, and I don't think Melchor is going to keep volunteering to give her his."

"We could search the other big cave," I said, getting excited.

"Let's do it!" Beau cried.

"We have to watch out for the guards," I said.

"What guards?" Beau asked.

"The ones who tied me up and put me in the pit," Kaye said.

"They found the ale in the cave house," I added.

"Oh," Beau said. "I'll go check on them." He was back in a few moments. "They're not going to bother us any time soon. They're too busy snoring."

"Let's be careful not to wake them up," Kaye said, taking my torch from me.

I was hungry again, so as soon as my hands were free, I fished around in my provision bag until I found some bread and cheese. I folded them together and took a big bite.

"Are you ready, Reggie?" Kaye asked, looking a little annoyed.

"We don't want to interrupt your meal," Beau said, laughing.

"Don't worry about me," I said. "I'll eat it on the way. Let's go."

We followed the tunnel to the other big cavern. Hurrying after the others, I tripped and went sprawling across the floor. I had fallen over the same pile of loose rock that I had stumbled over yesterday. I couldn't believe it! To make things worse, I had dropped my bread and cheese.

"Oh, Ratfingers," I whispered to myself. "Kaye, Beau," I called softly down the tunnel.

"What's wrong?" Kaye asked, turning back. "Are you hurt?"

"No," I said, getting to my knees. "I dropped my bread and cheese. I need the light to find it."

Both of them groaned, "Reggie!"

"What?" I said, still on the floor. "It won't take long. I can't look for treasure on an empty stomach." I looked up to see if they were really annoyed, but then I froze. "Look," I whispered, pointing upwards.

Someone had drawn a bird on the smooth, low ceiling of the tunnel.

"It's a falcon," Beau whispered.

"The treasure must be here somewhere," Kaye said. He examined the tunnel. "It's solid rock," he said, "except for the big heap of stones Reggie tripped on."

We looked at the pile of rocks. It was tall, heaped up against the wall of the tunnel. "It looks like part of the wall collapsed back there," Beau said.

"Maybe the treasure's behind it," I said excitedly.

"That's what I think," Kaye said. "This might not even be a real rockslide. Someone may have built it to hide the treasure."

"They did a good job," I said. "How are we supposed to get back there?"

"We move it," Kaye said.

"What?" I said. "How are we supposed to move a huge pile of rocks?"

Kaye grinned and stuck his torch in the pile so it would stay up. "One stone at a time," he said, grabbing a rock, carrying it a little farther up the tunnel, and starting a new rock pile against the wall.

"Let's get to work," Beau said, following Kaye's example.

I sighed and started moving rocks. Most of them were a good size for carrying, but there were a few really large stones in the pile too. I hoped we wouldn't have to move them all.

Our new pile grew steadily larger, and soon we had uncovered half of a small, square hole in the tunnel wall. If we squeezed through the narrow opening, the space was wide enough and high enough to crawl through, although it would have been hard for a grown-up.

Kaye lay on his stomach and poked a torch through the hole. "There's a room on the other side!" he whispered, his face lit up with excitement. "Let's go!"

He squirmed through the gap in the pile and disappeared into the wall. Beau and I soon followed.

I crept through the tiny passage and stood up in a good-sized room carved from the rock. It was filled from floor to ceiling with stacks of wooden boxes. A small path led through the middle of the stacks.

Kaye turned around, holding his light up high. "The treasure must be in these boxes!" he said, handing me the torch.

With Beau's help, he lifted one of the heavy boxes down, opened the latch and lifted the lid. The spark of bright gold caught the torchlight and brightened the gray, dusty room. Our eyes met above the shining pile of coins and we grinned at each other.

"We found it!" Kaye whispered.

"I can't believe it!" Beau said. After a moment he laughed and said, "Just think, we owe finding this treasure to bread and cheese."

I glared at Beau, but didn't say anything. Instead, I reached into the box and picked up a handful of coins, letting them trickle through my fingers with a tinkling sound. "Let's open up another one," I said, "just to make sure they're all full of treasure."

Kaye chose a box from a different stack. That one was filled with gems. Some glowed with rich colors and others sparkled with clear light. A third box gleamed with milky pearls, shining like cool drops of moonlight.

"Do you know what this means?" Kaye said. "I could still be a knight. The queen might not have paid Eldridge yet. I could still beat Melchor at his own game."

"You're right," I cried. "Those feasts can last for hours. Maybe they're still eating. Let's hurry."

"We have to show the queen," Beau said. "She'll be so relieved. Let's take some treasure back upstairs to prove we found it."

Kaye filled my bag with coins and jewels and gave it back to me. It was heavy, so I handed him the torch again. "This isn't a provision bag anymore," I joked. "It's a treasure bag." I opened it and looked inside, stirring the treasure with my hand. My fingers found something that didn't feel like treasure, and I pulled out a crust of bread. "Well, it's a treasure *and* provision bag, I guess," I said.

"Just don't accidentally nibble on a ruby," Beau joked. "Your teeth will break and we'll have to call you Gap-Mouth Reg."

"That sounds like a bandit name!" I said as we walked to the exit. "I *feel* like a bandit wearing all this treasure." After Kaye and Beau crept through the tiny passage, I followed them, pushing the treasure bag ahead of me as I crawled.

As I neared the end of the tunnel, I shoved the bag forward and said, "Beau, take this please." I began squeezing myself through the narrow gap in the pile of rocks. Beau grabbed the treasure bag and pulled it out. As he did so, its long strap caught between two rocks and tugged them loose.

They rolled down and landed on the tunnel floor near Beau's feet. Then I heard a noise like an angry beast awakening from sleep.

I turned my head and saw the rock pile bulge toward me like a giant wave, but even though it seemed to move so slowly, I couldn't get out of the way.

"Arrrgh!" I yelled, and I heard Beau and Kaye yelling too. I cringed and shut my eyes, pressing my face into the ground, ready to be smashed flat. I didn't see anything after that.

# chapter twenty-nine

"Reggie, are you dead? Wake up!" I heard a faraway voice talking, but I ignored it. I didn't want to wake up. Something was wrong. I liked being asleep. I had a bad feeling that if I woke up, that same something would start hurting very, very, badly.

A hand slapped my face. That wasn't fair! I didn't want to be slapped. It distracted me from trying to keep the hurt away.

"Reggie, please be okay!" Kaye whispered.

I felt another slap. I blinked.

"He's alive!" I heard voices shout. I blinked again and lifted my head a little bit. I saw Kaye and Beau. They looked scared and pale yellow, like dolls cut out of parchment.

I blinked some more and saw that Beau and Kaye were standing in the big tunnel. Only part of me was in the big tunnel. The rest of me was pinned under a pile of rocks.

"Owwww…" I whined.

"Can you move your legs?" Beau asked.

I tried. My legs were still inside the tiny tunnel. I could move them around easily.

"My legs are fine," I said. "It's just hard to breathe. The rocks are pressing down on me."

"We need to get help," Beau said. "I'll go find some."

"No!" I said. "Send Kaye for help. He can take the treasure and stay a knight." I looked at Beau. "Beau, give him the bag. Make him go."

Beau held the bag out to Kaye by one corner so it half-opened. Kaye stared at it. Two coins fell out, clinking and chiming as they bounced on the tunnel floor. In one motion, Kaye took the bag, bent over, and scooped up the two coins, dropping them back in the bag.

"Reggie—I don't think there's time for that," Kaye said, setting the bag down and starting to lift rocks off me. Beau joined him.

"Go!" I said. "Being a knight is so important to you."

"No," he said, picking up a big rock in his arms. "You're more important. All this time I've been so worried about staying a knight that I stopped acting like a knight. I'm sorry about that. I'm not going to make the same mistake now."

I laid my face down on the ground again. I was tired of holding it up. "What will you do if you can't be a knight? It's all you've ever dreamed of."

Kaye set down a rock and wiped his sleeve across his forehead. He shrugged and pulled another rock off me. "I don't know," he said. "I've never thought about what else I could do."

"You could be a gong farmer," Beau said, grabbing a rock in each hand and tossing them aside.

"Eww, no," I said. A gong farmer's job was to clean out the pits under the garderobes and privies. "He'd always smell worse than a dirty chamber pot. Kaye, you could go into the wool business with my father. He'd be honored to have you there."

Kaye smiled and rolled another rock off the pile. "Maybe I could raise horses."

"Do you know anything about raising horses?" Beau asked.

"No. But I can learn." Kaye laid down on the floor in front of me. "Look, Beau, this big slab of rock fell right across him. The only reason it didn't smash him is because this other rock is holding it up. If we can lift this up just a little, Reggie might be able to crawl out."

"It looks really heavy," Beau said. "We might need help."

"I'll help," a new voice said.

"Aaaagh!" we all yelled. My yell was not very loud. It was hard to get enough air in my lungs to make any noise.

An old woman stood in the tunnel. She wore a long gray cloak over a gray gown and carried a long pole.

Beau was the first to stop being surprised. "Good morrow, madam. Who are you?"

"I'm Reggie's friend," she answered. "My name is Agnes. I live here, but my house is a little crowded right now."

I gasped, or tried to. It sounded more like a hiccup. "You're my spook!"

She smiled. "And your friend. We have to get you out of here. I locked the guards in my house while they slept, but it won't take them long to break out of there. You've been loud enough to wake them by now. I can't believe the treasure was hidden so close to my house all this time and I never knew it."

Agnes showed Kaye and Beau how to use the pole as a lever to raise the big rock. When they lifted it, Agnes pulled me out. Her thin hands held mine with a strong grip. As soon as I was free, Beau and Kaye dropped the huge rock with a thump, and a new pile of rock rolled down, covering the entrance to the treasure room.

I sat up. I felt like I had been kicked in the ribs a hundred times, but other than that, I couldn't find much wrong with me. It felt good to breathe again.

"Take a really deep breath, Reggie," Beau said. "Do you feel any stabbing pains?"

I sucked air deep into my chest and shook my head.

"That's good," Beau said. "You might not have broken anything. Time will tell. Can you walk?"

Kaye helped me to my feet. I felt shaky, but everything seemed to work. I had just taken a few experimental steps when a crashing, tearing noise echoed down the tunnel.

"That will be the guards," Agnes said. "Let's go. If they see you with that treasure, they'll never let you out of here."

Beau grabbed the treasure bag and our last flickering torch and sprinted toward the stairs. We raced after him, up the tunnel and up the stairs. I could hear the guards shouting and cursing as they stumbled through the tunnel.

At the top of the stairs, I leaned against the wall, panting for air, which really hurt my poor ribs. Beau grabbed the loop of rope on the door to the mews and gave it a sharp tug. Nothing happened. He pulled again, but the door didn't budge.

"If I didn't know better," he said, "I'd say the door is locked."

"Let me try," Kaye said. He couldn't open it either. "It's blocked on the other side," he said.

I heard a distant yell. "I think they figured out you escaped from the pit," I said.

"It won't take them long to find us now," Beau said. "Should we try to hide in one of the caves until they pass and then go out the back way?"

"No," Agnes said, taking the torch from Beau. "Follow me." She led us back down the stairs. At the bottom she bent down and pulled a lever hidden in a crack on the floor. With a loud crunching noise, a thin, dark gap appeared in the wall, running from floor to ceiling. Agnes grabbed the edge of the gap and silently swung a whole section of the wall open like a door.

"Get in, quickly," she said.

Agnes followed us into the dark and heaved the wall closed again with a tremendous crash. She chuckled. "That noise will give them something to wonder about."

# CHAPTER THIRTY

"Where are we?" I asked.

"*In* the castle. Inside the wall. Follow me."

She led us along a passage so narrow I bounced from wall to wall. The air felt close and still and so thick it was hard to breathe. My palms grew slick with sweat, and I felt big drops of it sliding down the sides of my face. I lifted a hand to wipe my face and had to turn sideways to do it. Ahead of me, Agnes held the torch up high, looking frail and slightly stooped in her fluttering gray cloak.

"How do you know about all these hidden passages, Agnes?" I asked.

She glanced over her shoulder at me. "I grew up in this castle—with King Frederic, my husband Phillip, and Alfred. We knew all the castle's secrets."

"Alfred? You mean Old Stone Face?" I cried.

Agnes shook her head at me. "Why would you call poor Alfred a name like that? I expect better from you boys."

"He never talks," I said. "Never. And he never smiles. Sometimes he grunts."

"It's true." I heard Beau's voice come from far behind me.

Agnes sighed. "Poor Alfred. He took the king's death to heart. Blames himself. I remember him as a boy. He talked all the time. Even talked in his sleep, I was told."

"Why doesn't Alfred use the secret passages too?" I asked.

"I don't know," Agnes said. "Maybe he doesn't want to be reminded of his old friends who are gone now."

I looked back at Kaye and Beau and raised my eyebrows. They shrugged. "Who knew?" Kaye whispered.

Turning back around to follow Agnes, I banged my arm into the wall, which jostled my tender ribs.

"Ow!" I cried. "Maybe Alfred doesn't come down here because he's too big to fit."

Agnes laughed. It was dry, and sounded almost like a cough, but it had a nice sound to it anyway.

I had one more question. "Agnes, remember when you drew the arrow in the dust on the library table for us? If you didn't know where the treasure was, how did you know we needed to look inside the falcon carving in the library?"

"I listened to the queen's council meeting," she said. "Afterward, I overheard you say the clue was a falcon with a funny eye and I knew exactly what that meant. When we were children, the king and Alfred and Phillip and I used the one-eyed falcon carving to leave each other messages and treats all the time."

"You hid in *that* wall?" I asked. "You listened to my story about the dragon, didn't you? I heard you laugh!"

She chuckled. "I couldn't help it. It's been a long time since I heard a good story around here."

"How did you get into the library to leave the sweet and draw the clue in the dust?" I asked.

"I can hide in the wall behind the library too," she said. "I heard you having a bad day, so I left you a sweet. There's an opening in the wall, if you look hard enough."

Kaye huffed behind me and muttered, "We didn't have time to check the library walls."

The passage turned into stairs almost as steep as a ladder. I stopped asking questions because I was panting like a dog in the sun. My ribs hurt with every breath I drew.

Just when I couldn't take it anymore, the stairs ended, and Agnes stopped next to a wooden panel set low in the wall. The narrow passage continued beyond her. I saw more stairs ahead, this time tiny and spiraling upward like a stretched out snail shell.

"Where does that go?" I asked, pointing at the curling stairs.

"Up," she said. "Up to the hall where you found my footprints. I had to clean it so you wouldn't find me. I didn't know I could trust you then, and that was my best view of the courtyard. It gets lonely in the caves. Sometimes it's nice to come out and see people, even through a window."

I slapped my forehead. "I can't believe I never looked across the hall! The footprints had to come from somewhere." I sighed and looked back at Kaye. "You would have thought of that."

"Maybe," he said, "but I should have listened to you when you tried to tell me about the footprints. Anyway, I don't think we would have found the treasure any faster by coming this way."

Agnes stooped down, took hold of the wooden panel, and slid it upwards. I got down on my knees and found myself staring into the surprised eyes of Tom Spot as he paused in the middle of scurrying around the kitchen.

"Ratfingers, Master Reggie! How did you get inside the wall?" Tom cried.

We crawled into the kitchen, which felt gloriously cool after that stuffy passage. "Meet our spook, Tom," I said. "Her name is Agnes. We found the treasure too."

Tom bobbed a bow, but Kaye grabbed his arm. "Is the feast over? Did the queen pay the Eldridge people yet?"

"The feast's still on," Tom said. "Master Abelard started making some special sweets, on account of the king of Eldridge being here."

"What? The king himself came?" Beau asked.

"Aye. No one expected him, so we've all been chasing our tails trying to make everything good enough for a visiting king."

"But the queen—has she paid him Melchor's money yet?" Kaye asked again.

"Yes," Tom said. "She paid him when we brought in the roast venison. The queen wanted to wait until the feast was over, but the king of Eldridge wanted it right away. He's a stubborn one. Seems cross too. He's got his money sitting in boxes in there where he can keep an eye on it."

"Is Melchor in there?" I asked.

Tom nodded.

"Then we're too late," I said. I wanted to cry. My chest hurt so much and all the hard work we had done—getting Kaye out of the pit, finding the treasure, getting buried under rocks, racing up a few hundred steps—had been for nothing.

"We already knew that," Kaye said. "The queen still needs the treasure. Let's go give it to her and tell them all a tale they've never heard before."

"He's right," Beau said. "Kaye might as well give everyone something good to remember him by." He handed me the treasure bag.

"But Melchor's really going to enjoy it if the queen removes you from being a knight in front of everyone *and* the king of Eldridge," I said.

Kaye made a face. "I know. Let's just finish this."

"Go ahead," Agnes said. "Be brave. I'll be here if you need me."

# chapter thirty-one

Kaye took a deep breath and walked out of the kitchen. Beau and I followed him into the great hall, where two lines of white-covered tables ran the length of the entire hall. At the far end, the queen dined with her important guests at a raised table facing the rest of the room.

We walked the whole length of the room to reach the queen. Everyone stared. I glanced at Kaye and Beau. They looked filthy, like they had been carrying rocks. Dirt streaked their clothing and skin. Dust from the rock fall coated their hair, making them as gray as old grandfathers. Smears of grime striped their faces and a dark trickle ran from Kaye's cheek down to his chin, like a muddy tear.

I must have looked worse, since I had been the one under the rock pile. I hugged the treasure bag close to my stomach with both arms. The strap dangled down to my ankles. I tucked it up. The last thing I needed was to trip again in front of all these people.

With every step we took toward the queen, little waves of silence spread out from us across the room, like we were pebbles tossed into a pond. The queen lifted her hand and the musicians in the gallery quieted their instruments and leaned over the railing to see what was happening.

Kaye's steps didn't falter as he drew near the queen. We knelt before her in a triangle shape—Kaye in front and Beau and I behind him. I glanced up and saw Melchor sitting at the queen's left hand, barely holding back a gloating grin. A thin man with a big hooked nose sat at the queen's right hand. His small black eyes shone as bright as a beetle's shell. He had to be King Aldric of Eldridge.

"What's this?" the king grumbled, peering at us with his bright, beady eyes. "Is this some troupe of acrobats you found in a ditch somewhere, Vianne? I hope they're better than the ones that just left."

"Rise, Sir Kaye, Your Grace, and Master Reggie," the queen said. We stood. The queen smiled and said to the king of Eldridge, "No, Aldric. This is one of the knights of my realm, the noble Sir Kaye."

"He seems undersized," the king muttered. "Don't you feed your knights here in Knox?"

Melchor smiled with enjoyment like a cat full of stolen cream.

Platters heaped with food covered the table in front of the queen. The king picked up his beautiful pearl-handled eating knife, carved off a chunk of roast venison and offered it to Kaye on the point of the knife. "Here, boy, you look like you need some meat for your bones."

The queen laid a hand on the king's arm and said, "In a moment, Aldric. These boys look like they have an interesting story to tell."

"Then let them tell it," he said with a frown. "We need something to pass the time. Why is your kitchen so slow about sending out the sweets?"

"The sweets will be worth waiting for," the queen said. "Our cook Abelard never disappoints." She nodded to Kaye. "Proceed, Sir Kaye."

Kaye bowed to the two rulers. "Your Majesty," he said to the queen, "I have completed my quest and found the lost treasure of Castle Forte."

Melchor began to laugh. "How do we know he's not lying?" he said. "Where's the proof?"

Kaye glanced at me over his shoulder. Angry at Melchor, I marched right up to the table, climbed onto the platform, and dumped out everything in my bag in front of the queen. A glittering cascade of gold and gems poured across the table, followed by a dried apple slice and two raisin tarts.

"There's more where that came from!" I said to Melchor. "Lots more!"

Melchor was quiet. He looked like his gut was giving him pains. Then, staring at Kaye with a hateful look in his eyes and spitting out the words like they tasted bad, he said, "It doesn't matter. You're too late. You're not a knight anymore."

We all looked at the queen. "I'm afraid it's true, Kaye," she said softly. "I'm sorry. I tried to wait as long as I could to pay King Aldric."

Kaye's head drooped.

"Wait a moment," King Aldric said, taking a bite of something in his hand.

Suspicious of the careful way he held the food, I stared at him closely. I couldn't figure out what he held, but when I looked at the pile of treasure again, I blinked with surprise. One of the raisin tarts was gone. My gaze snapped back to the king. He had pinched my raisin tart!

Aldric cleared a crumb from his throat. "Vianne," he said, "do you mean to say that this boy has found a lost treasure—and as a reward, you are taking away his knighthood?"

"It's not a reward," the queen said sadly. "It was a wager that Kaye lost." She explained the terms of the agreement to the king. He listened carefully, occasionally nibbling on his stolen tart.

When the queen finished, Aldric leaned across the table and fixed his sharp gaze on Kaye. "Young man, if I were you, I'd refuse to tell the queen where the rest of the treasure is unless she lets you stay a knight."

Kaye smiled and shook his head. "Thank you, Your Majesty, but whether I am a knight or not, I still serve the queen. She needs the treasure to run her kingdom. I agreed to the terms of the wager, and I lost. I was too late."

The king leaned back in his chair, lightly smacking his empty lips together. I saw his glance fall on the last raisin tart. I frowned hard at him and then turned to the queen. "Please, Your Majesty," I begged. "Kaye tried so hard. It's not his fault he was late. He and Beau had to rescue me from under a rockslide. And before that, he was tied up in a hole in the ground all night until Beau and I found him today."

Queen Vianne laid both her hands flat on the table in front of her and looked at them. It took me a moment to realize she was angry but trying not to show it. When she lifted her eyes again, she was calm. "There seems to be more to this story than I've been told. Who tied up Kaye?" She looked at Melchor. "Was it you?"

He shook his head in surprise. "No, not at all."

The queen narrowed her eyes. "Was it done by someone else, under your orders?"

"No!" he shouted. "I never thought he'd find the treasure. No one's been able to find it. I was sure he would lose the bet all by himself. By my life, I swear I did nothing to him."

The queen ignored him. She beckoned Nicolette over and whispered to her. Nicolette left the room and the queen said, "Melchor, you were the one most eager to stop Kaye from being a knight. Your dislike for him is well-known. I hope you remember the punishment I promised to anyone who harmed Kaye in any way. Are you prepared to lose your knighthood and your lands? Because I find it hard to believe you could tie Kaye up and leave him at the bottom of a hole without hurting him at all."

Melchor looked confused. "No, upon my word, I tell you I had nothing to do with this. I'm innocent!" he cried. I actually believed him.

Milo stood up, a cup in his hand. He had been sitting at one of the long tables, not far from Beau. "Your Majesty, don't take Melchor's lands. He didn't do anything. I did. Melchor knew nothing about it. And I never hurt him," he said, jerking his head toward Kaye.

Nicolette returned with a parchment. It was the parchment that Melchor and the queen had signed at the meeting of the knights. I saw their seals hanging off the edge of the document when the queen took it from Nicolette.

"I'm glad you are above such petty trickery, Melchor," she said. "But this changes things. Kaye will remain a knight."

Kaye lifted his face to the queen, full of hope and a thousand questions, but she kept her attention focused on Melchor.

Melchor sputtered and said, "But he was too late. I provided the money to pay Eldridge. The agreement was that if I did that, Kaye would no longer be a knight."

The queen studied the parchment carefully and said, "I will of course repay your money, Sir Melchor. I thank you for being

willing to provide it in order to prevent a war that would have brought much suffering to both countries."

The king had the good sense to blush a little when he heard that. Queen Vianne ran a finger down the lines of writing. Her finger stopped. "Here," she said. "It clearly says that if anyone should try to harm Kaye or prevent him from finding the treasure, the conditions of this agreement will no longer apply—which means that if anyone tried to stop Kaye from finding the treasure, Kaye would not lose his knighthood. See for yourself," she added, handing the parchment to Melchor.

He stared at the spot on the page that she pointed to for a while. I had never seen Melchor with nothing to say. Finally, he set the parchment down on the table between himself and the queen.

"You signed it yourself," the queen said, "and affixed your seal to it. You agreed to those conditions."

Melchor nodded slowly. Then he looked at Milo, who still stood with the cup in his hand, looking foolish. "Why would you do this?" he said in a voice so deep I heard it rumble in his chest.

Milo jumped. A splash of wine fell on his boots. "I—I was trying to help. I thought if I kept him out of the way, he couldn't ruin your big day."

"No," Melchor said. "*You're* the one who ruined it." Milo turned pale. Melchor wiped his lips and took a sip of wine. "I would like to speak with you, Milo," he said. "Outside." Melchor inclined his head to the queen, "By your leave, of course, Your Majesty," he asked.

The queen nodded and Melchor rose. Milo bowed to the queen and walked toward the exit. Melchor strolled behind him. Together, they moved faster and faster, until Milo was running out to the courtyard as Melchor chased after him.

# chapter thirty-two

Queen Vianne chuckled. "That worked out well. Thank you, Kaye, for finding the treasure."

Kaye bowed. "You're welcome, Your Majesty. But I'm the one who must thank you. I didn't want to stop being a knight. How—how did you get Melchor to sign that parchment?"

The queen dropped her voice low and beckoned Beau and Kaye to climb up next to me on the platform. "Melchor doesn't read very well," she whispered, "but I knew he'd be too proud to admit it in front of all the other knights. Instead, he signed the parchment without knowing what it said. I don't think he'll do that again in a hurry."

I pulled in a deep breath of relief, feeling all my sore bones stretch and crackle. Everything had worked out for the best. As I exhaled, I glanced down and saw a lonely slice of dried apple sitting on top of the treasure. The king had taken my last tart while everyone watched Melchor and Milo! I gave him a stern look, but he just blinked his round button eyes at me like he hadn't done anything wrong.

King Aldric turned to the queen. "I feel that there is more to this story," he said. "And since the kitchen still hasn't sent out any sweets, we might as well hear the rest of it. I know who Sir Kaye is." He gestured toward Beau. "That one, I assume, is your nephew the duke." Then he pointed at me. "Who is the extra-dirty one? Another duke or knight? Maybe a small king of somewhere?"

"No, this is Reginald Stork," the queen said. "Reggie for short."

The king gave me a sharp, sideways look, like a bird might. "Just Reggie, eh? Well, what does he do? Other than collect dirt?"

I felt the whole room staring at my dusty back. I blushed and looked down, realizing that without noticing, I had taken my bead out of my pocket and already held it tightly in my hand.

"Everything, Your Majesties," Kaye said. "He does everything. I will tell you a tale."

Kaye lifted his voice, and the whole room listened. He told about all the things I did and all the clues I found that led us to the treasure.

Soon the kitchen boys carried out plates of fruit and cheese and sweets. When Embert slid a big dish of raisin tarts between the king and the queen, I sighed. They smelled so good, and I was so hungry, but I knew I wouldn't get to eat until Kaye finished the story. From where I stood, I had a fine view of the king as he ate seventeen tarts during Kaye's tale.

Kaye even told about how mean he was to Beau and me, but that we found him and rescued him anyway. When he told how we moved the rocks and found the treasure room, he said, "Reggie's the one who found the clue that marked the treasure room. We never would have found it without Reggie. He's the real hero! Three cheers for Reggie!"

"Hooray! Hooray! Hooray!" cried everyone in the room, waving their cups and bits of their dinner in the air. Beau put his hands around his mouth and shouted louder than anyone. Kaye kept grinning while he shouted. Behind Kaye, a man as big as a bear stood smiling by the door. When he caught my eye, he bowed in my direction. Embert shouted with all his might, his eyes shut and his hands clenched into fists at his sides. The

two Toms jumped in the air and waved their arms. Even some of the dogs barked with excitement. My cheeks burned so hot, I worried the dirt on my face might catch fire.

The queen laughed at my red face, but in a friendly way. She gestured to the minstrels to begin playing again. Everyone went back to eating. Under the noise of music and conversation, the king of Eldridge said, "Vianne, I thought you'd gone mad when I heard you had knighted Henry's child, but it seems to be going well. Maybe you should knight this one too. He seems a useful sort of person."

My mouth popped open and I stared at him for a moment before shouting, "No!" I clapped my hand over my mouth and dropped to the ground to kneel in apology. I couldn't believe I had contradicted a king. I heard Beau chuckle and dared to look up. All I could see was the white tablecloth in front of me.

"Please stand, Reggie," the queen said. "It's hard to see you down there."

I liked hiding behind the table, but I stood up and said, "I apologize, Majesties."

The queen smiled. "Of course, Reggie. You really don't wish to be a knight? You've shown great courage, valor, and loyalty. These are fine qualities for a knight."

I blushed again. "Thank you, Your Majesty, but I'd be a terrible knight. I always say the wrong thing. I'm clumsy. I'd probably stab myself with a sword by accident, and I don't get along with horses very well."

"There's more to being a knight than skill with swords and horses," the queen said.

"Yes, Your Majesty," I said, "but swords and horses are important too."

"Well then, boy, if you don't want to be a knight, what do you want to be?" the king asked.

"I don't know, Your Majesty," I said. "I don't know what I'm good at—or if I'm good at anything."

"What do you like to do?" the queen asked. "If you like doing something, you're probably good at it."

No one had ever asked me that before, but the queen was really listening, so I shrugged and said, "I like exploring and finding things. I like collecting the things I find. I like talking to nice people and finding out about them. I like telling stories." I thought for a moment. "I like helping Kaye when *he's* being a knight."

"Reggie tells good tales," Beau said. "He always makes me laugh."

"Ah," the king said thoughtfully, "perhaps you would make a good chronicler."

"What's that?" I asked.

"A chronicler is a kind of historian. They go places and see things happening. They talk to people and collect true tales. Then they write them down for people to read and learn from. You would be good at that, I think," the king said.

I liked the sound of that. He was right. I would be good at all of that—except the writing down part.

Kaye knew what I was thinking. "You like the book about Sir Gregory," he said. "Someone had to write those stories down."

"But why can't I just tell people my tales?" I asked. "Then they could tell other people and soon everyone would know."

"People forget," the king said. "When they tell stories, they change them. If you write down the things that happen to you and your friends, people will remember the truth about your lives."

"But I can't write!" I cried out. "I'm terrible at it."

The king shrugged and selected another tart from the dish next to him. "If you really want to do it, you'll find a way."

"Do you want to find a way, Reggie?" the queen asked me.

I bit my lip and squeezed my hands together, thinking hard. "Do you think I can?" I asked the queen in a voice that only she could hear. She smiled into my eyes and gave a quick, firm nod. I wasn't as confident as she was, but I said, "I will try, Your Majesty."

Her smile widened. "Then I will make you the Royal Chronicler of Knox. You will record your adventures with Sir Kaye and His Grace the Duke so that everyone can know your stories. You will receive five gold coins each month and you will always have a home in the castle."

Kaye chuckled and said, "Finally, something to put in your pigge pot, Reggie."

Five gold coins a month! I'd be rich in no time. My father would be so impressed that he—"Do you know what this means?" I cried.

"No. What does it mean?" the king asked, looking suspicious.

"My father's never going to try and make me learn the wool business ever again!"

# chapter thirty-three

Finally, we got to eat. It was late. The feast was over. The minstrels packed up their instruments and left. Nicolette scurried about, showing important guests to their rooms. She came for the king, lifting her candle holder high to light the way. He bid us good night and followed Nicolette.

They paused by the door to speak to the big bear-like man and continued on their way. I helped myself to more roast venison and the rest of the raisin tarts. I thought I deserved them after my long day.

Now that the important guests were gone, the queen closed her eyes and leaned back in her chair. Although much improved, she still looked pale and tired after being sick yesterday.

I glanced at the big man by the door again. He seemed familiar, but I didn't know him. I poked Kaye. "Who's that?" I asked.

He took a big bite of apricot and looked where I was pointing. The fruit fell from his fingers. Kaye swallowed hard. The next moment, he scrambled out of his chair and flew across the hall to the big man. He leaped into the man's arms and stayed there, talking so fast. The man looked like he'd never get tired of listening to Kaye or of holding onto him.

Beau sat down next to me, a funny look on his face. "Sir Henry," he said.

I nodded, watching them closely. After a long time, I said, "I don't think my father's ever been that happy to hear me talk."

"I hope my children will like me that much," Beau said.

Surprised, I said, "I didn't know you thought about children."

"I have to," he said. "If my aunt doesn't have children, someday the throne of Knox will pass to me and my children."

"The queen might still marry and have children," I said.

"Maybe," he said, "but she mourns my uncle. She thinks it would be hard to marry again."

"Wait—she was married?" I asked in a shocked whisper.

Beau nodded. "To the uncle I told you about—the one who died in a hunting accident."

"I thought you meant some other uncle! I never realized he was married to the queen."

"Yes," Beau said, "but he's gone now. We both miss him. I always wished he was my real father."

In silence, we watched Sir Henry find a chair, sit on it, and put Kaye on his knee, listening to Kaye's chatter with a proud smile on his face. At one point, he threw back his head and laughed. I hoped Kaye wasn't talking about me. Beau sighed.

I looked at him and said, "You don't have to worry about being a good father. You're already a good friend. That's halfway there."

"Thanks," he said. Then he wrinkled his eyebrows. "You aren't going to write this down in one of your history books, are you?"

"Maybe I will and maybe I won't," I teased him. "But even if I do, no one will be able to read my writing."

He laughed out loud. One of the dogs sleeping in a pile at the other end of the hall lifted her head at the sound, but she went right back to sleep. While I watched the dog, I noticed Agnes peeping into the room.

"Oh!" I said. "We forgot to introduce Agnes to the queen."

"I'll do it," Beau said, and ran to offer Agnes his arm.

Watching them approach the queen, I suddenly felt sorry for both of them, and not just because they were dirty and tired.

I thought about Agnes, who had been hiding in the dark for months, lonely, afraid for her life, and always missing her husband. Then I thought about Beau, who missed his uncle and feared growing up to be like his father.

Looking around the room, I saw the queen, who missed her husband so much that she made herself sick staying up night after night to paint his portrait. I only had to glance at Kaye to see how much he missed his father all the time. I thought of Alfred, who blamed himself for the king's death so much that he stopped talking. Even Abelard in the kitchen loved the queen but couldn't do anything about it.

A thought struck my brain like lightning, but unlike lightning, the brightness of the thought stayed with me. Maybe everyone carried some kind of sadness hidden inside them. Maybe that's why my mum wanted me to be kind to everyone—because she knew that it's really mean to hurt someone who's already hurting inside.

I shook my head and blinked a few times. I needed to think more about this when I wasn't so tired.

Beau introduced Agnes to the queen, and Sir Henry and Kaye joined us. Sir Henry knew Agnes. He wrapped his big arm around her shoulder and hugged her.

"Faithful Agnes," he said. "Kaye tells me you've been living in a house under the castle, but you've been keeping an eye on everything, just like always. How did you come to live in the caves after the king died?"

Agnes leaned against Sir Henry and said, "Some of the knights threw me out of the castle after King Frederic died," she said.

"Phillip was afraid that might happen, so long before he died, he prepared a home for me in the caverns. He wanted me to have a safe place to stay if I ever needed one."

"Your husband was a wise and cautious man," the queen said.

Agnes caught her breath. "Not cautious enough. He couldn't save the king or himself. We knew someone was making the king ill. We suspected poison, but even by keeping his medicines locked away and preparing all his food myself, we couldn't save him."

Sir Henry tightened his arm around Agnes and said, "You tried. You were the king's loyal friends to the very end."

Agnes' eyes grew bright with tears, but she did not cry. "After they threw me out, I used my knowledge of the castle to creep back in and spy on them. I had to find out who had killed Phillip and the king. If I had only done that sooner, I might have prevented their deaths." Now the tears dropped down her cheeks.

After a moment, the queen asked, "What did you discover?"

"There were three knights plotting against the king—Sir Fangle, Sir Dworfurd, and Sir Bragwayne. Fangle and Bragwayne were the ones who threw me out after the king died."

Sir Henry released Agnes and stared into her face. "The knights from Abegnayle?" he said. "Please, tell me everything you know about them."

"They're gone now. Sir Fangle died of a terrible cough. I played tricks on Sir Bragwayne until he thought the castle was haunted and ran away. I helped expose Sir Dworfurd's bad deeds, and he was imprisoned, but now he's escaped. They poisoned the king, just enough to make him sick for a long time—so sick he wouldn't be able to pay attention to everything happening in Knox. They were hiding something from the king and wanted to keep him distracted."

"What were they hiding?" Beau asked.

Agnes shook her head. "I couldn't find that out. All I know is that it was something they hoped would make them very rich."

"But what could make them rich only as long as the king didn't know about it?" Kaye asked. "Wool smuggling?"

"I don't know," Agnes said, "but they were determined that Queen Vianne would never know their secret either. That's why Dworfurd destroyed King Frederic's papers, Your Majesty. I unlocked the door behind him when he thought he was safe. That's how your tutor caught him in the act!"

"Alchir may have seen what was written on the documents before they burned up. Perhaps he knows the secret they were trying to hide," the queen said.

"Where is Alchir? Can we ask him?" Sir Henry asked.

The queen shook her head. "He's not here. He left yesterday to meet his daughter, who is journeying here from Vinland."

"He traveled alone?" Sir Henry asked.

The queen nodded. "I offered him a guard, but he said he would travel faster alone."

Sir Henry shook his head. "If he knows Dworfurd's secret and Dworfurd has escaped, Alchir's life may be in danger. It might be wise to send some knights to protect him and his daughter, Your Majesty."

I saw a spark in Kaye's eyes. I had a feeling he planned to be one of those knights.

"I was thinking the same thing," the queen said. "Would you be willing to join the search?"

"I'm sorry, Your Majesty," Sir Henry said. "King Aldric returns to Eldridge tomorrow. He fears to leave his kingdom for too long. There are trouble-makers hard at work in Eldridge too. I am afraid they might have been working with the three knights who killed King Frederic. I need to find out more, so I must return with the king."

Kaye's face fell, but he didn't say anything. Nicolette entered the hall, having finally shown the last of the important guests to their rooms. Alfred stumped slowly along behind her, holding a big ring of keys in his hands, his eyes on the ground. Long before Alfred reached us, Nicolette had settled into a chair with a sigh. As soon as Nicolette set down the heavy candleholder, Agnes darted forward and blew out Nicolette's candles with two sharp puffs of air.

Waving the smoke away with her hands, she said in a voice loud with fear, "*Never* use those candles. The big ones marked with the royal seal are poisoned. When the candles burn, the poison goes into the air, where people can breathe it in. It killed the king. I heard the knights from Abegnayle talking about it after the king died. I never thought the candles were still being used."

The queen looked shocked. Nicolette began to cry. "I *told* you that painting late at night was making you sick," she sobbed to the queen. "You wouldn't listen to me! How many candles did you burn?"

"Too many," the queen said, with a tremor in her voice.

Beau put his arm around Queen Vianne and pulled her close. "I'm glad we found out before it was too late," he said.

Agnes looked away from them and caught sight of Alfred. "Alfred!" she cried out.

Alfred's head snapped up and he dropped the keys. They vanished into the rushes underfoot with a soft jangle. Alfred took a few steps forward and Agnes ran to him, throwing her arms around his neck. Very stiffly, he folded his arms around her and stood there like a statue as Agnes cried into his shoulder.

Alfred moved his jaws up and down. Then, with a voice that rasped like grasshopper noise in midsummer, Alfred creaked out the word, "Agnes," and patted her back. We stared at him. Even three of the dogs stood up and looked his way.

Agnes stepped back and took a good look at him. "They said you stopped talking, Alfred."

He nodded, but didn't say anything else. Beau and Kaye and I looked at each other and tried not to laugh.

Queen Vianne said, "I will bid you good night. It's late, my friends. Tomorrow we have much to do. The king and his company will be returning to Eldridge. I must organize some knights to search for Alchir and his daughter. Sir Henry, I would like to meet with you tomorrow before you leave."

"Of course, Your Majesty," he said with a bow as she and Nicolette left the room. Agnes still spoke quietly to Alfred, who nodded and grunted occasionally.

Finally, Sir Henry looked at Kaye and Beau and me and gave a great big yawn, so that all of us yawned too. "I see you are all as tired as I am," he said, making us laugh, "but perhaps you could come upstairs and tell me the rest of your adventures before I have to leave again—especially you, Reggie. I want to hear more about Spook Agnes of Castle Forte."

"Of course we'll come," Kaye said, pulling his father toward the doorway by the arm. Beau and I grinned at each other and ran to catch up with them. I couldn't believe it. I had told so many stories about Sir Henry to other people, and now I was actually going to tell a story to Sir Henry himself—and this time, the story was going to be about me!

# acknowledgements

I would like to express my sincere appreciation and special thanks to Bob Lawson, David Ciambrone, Garrison Martt, Kathy Kerr, Lynne Holder, Ron Braley, and Susannah Cord. All of you were so helpful in assisting me with the medieval research that went into the making of this book and I am very grateful for your encouragement and support.

# about the author

Don M. Winn is the award-winning author of ten children's picture books, including *Superhero*, *The Higgledy-Piggledy Pigeon*, *Twitch the Squirrel and the Forbidden Bridge*, and *Space Cop Zack, Protector of the Galaxy*.

*The Lost Castle Treasure* is his second novel for middle readers and the sequel to *The Knighting of Sir Kaye*.

Don currently lives with his family in Round Rock, Texas.

Visit his website at **www.donwinn.com** for more information and all the latest news. If you liked this book, he'd love to hear from you.

You can e-mail him at **author@donwinn.com**.

Don't miss Sir Kaye the Boy Knight® Book One:
*The Knighting of Sir Kaye*

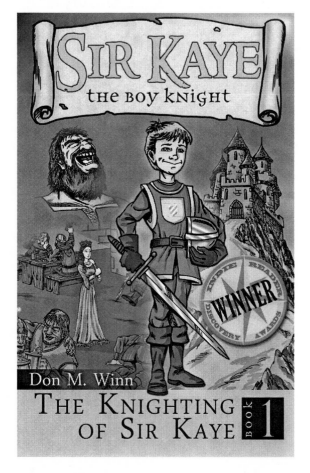

**An IndieReader Discovery Award Winner**
**A Moonbeam Children's Book Award Winner**

"A lively and adventurous kids' book, full of gentle humor and warmth." — *IndieReader Review*

"A fantastic, fun-filled adventure. Highly recommended."
— *The Wishing Shelf Book Award, Silver Medal Winner*

Look for Sir Kaye the Boy Knight® Book Three:
*Legend of the Forest Beast*

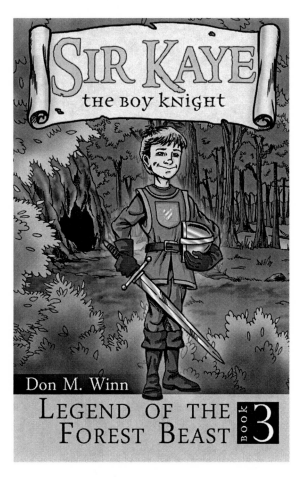

Kaye's tutor is missing! Kaye, Reggie, and Beau
set out to find him. Vanishing sheep, rumors
of a mysterious beast, and one very determined
girl make this an adventure of a lifetime.

CPSIA information can be obtained at www.ICGtesting.com
Printed in the USA
LVOW06s0214290815

452024LV00002B/199/P